The Wind

Tales from a Revolution: West-Florida

The Wind

Lars D. H. Hedbor

Yvonne Welch Brod

Brief Candle
Press

Cover and book design: Brief Candle Press
Cover image based on "The Shipwreck," Claude Joseph Vernet, 1772
Map reproductions courtesy of the Darlington Digital Library at the University of Pittsburgh, and the Library of Congress, Geography and Map Division.
Fonts: Allegheney, Doves Type and IM FELL English.

First Brief Candle Press edition published 2015
www.briefcandlepress.com

ISBN: 978-1-942319-16-0

Dedication

for Lara,
who showed me
the first step
on the path

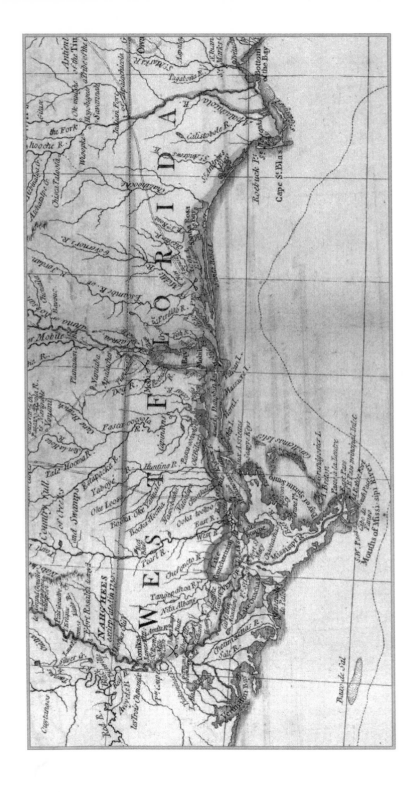

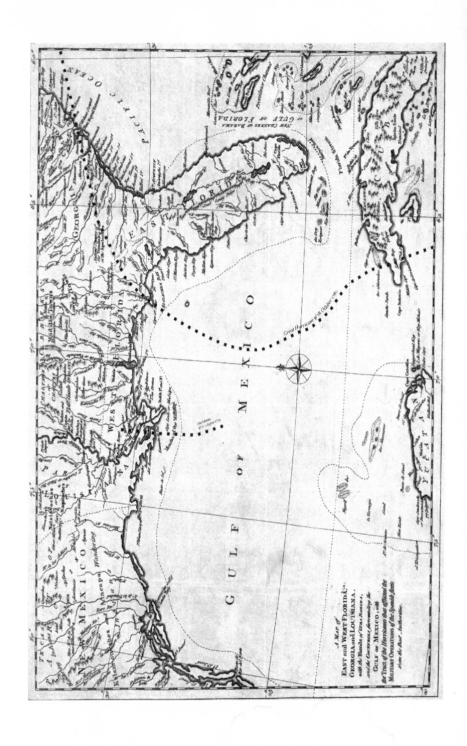

A Map of
EAST and WEST FLORIDA,
GEORGIA and LOUISIANA,
with the Bands of East, Bahama,
and the Continent, surrounding the
GULF of MEXICO, with
the Track of the Hurricane that affected the
Military Operations of the Spanish forces
from the East Indians.

Chapter I

As he sank beneath the waves, Gabriel found himself becoming very calm. The water was warm, and it was quiet down here—quiet, at least, in comparison to the chaos that reigned above.

The whistling of the wind in the rigging, the desperate shouts of men struggling to make themselves heard over the storm, the crash of water against the sides of the ship, all were silenced. Gone, too, were the cracks and thuds of falling spars, the hoarse cries of surprise wrenched from the throats of men as they were swept from the decks, and the deep, muffled booms of thunder.

It was not an unbroken peace, however. Gabriel was aware of pain, both in the leg that had caught awkwardly on the railing as he went overboard, and growing in his lungs, as his breath ran out.

Calm was replaced with a growing sense of concern, even panic, and he would ever after this day remember the moment when he realized that he had a choice, a decision to make. Decades hence, he would relate to his grandchildren the moment when he realized that he had decided to live, although he'd never be able to clearly explain what had driven him to the decision.

Although a single, sharply painful kick proved that his injured leg was not fit for propelling himself, he began to kick with his good leg, and struggled toward the surface on the strength of his arms and his will.

By the time he broke the surface, his lungs burned as if he'd inhaled the smoke of burning pitch, and his first breath was more water than air, it seemed. It was enough to win him a second surfacing, and another coughing breath, and then another. He finally gained the strength to stay above water long enough to see that his ship, scarcely more than a wallowing river barge under the best of circumstances, was heeled over sharply.

He noted that its mainmast had been carried off by the force of the wind on just the sheets of rigging, and guessed that the supplies he'd helped painstakingly load and balance in the hold now laid against the starboard side, dooming her to list until she should founder and go down. As there was no prospect of rescue from that quarter, he turned his attention in the opposite direction, where he could just make out the lights of shore.

Not for the first time, he sent a blessing heavenward to his father, thanking him for forcing his eldest son to learn how to swim. "The day will come, *mi hijo*, when you shall have the choice of whether to sink or to swim," he'd said, and it looked to Gabriel as though this day were the one. Turning away from the sight of the sinking ship, he struck out for the shoreline illuminated by lightning, pulling himself along with his arms. As he swam, he gritted his teeth and did his best to ignore the pain of his damaged leg.

An eternity later, he cried out as he was lifted by a breaking wave and driven heavily into the gravel of the shore. He tumbled in the surf for a few minutes, his injured leg bringing him fresh agonies each time it was bashed into something or twisted by the swirling waves, but finally found a moment when he was deposited on relatively dry ground long enough to pull himself clear of the water entirely.

The wind, which had been devilishly rising throughout the day, seemed to be whipping itself into an even higher frenzy now, and a flash of lightning revealed the hulk of a ship—whether it was his or another he could not tell—being rolled up into the shattered embrace of a copse of live oak, a mere dozen paces from where he lay.

The sight galvanized him into action, as he realized that although he was no longer actively engaged in the process of drowning, he was far from any sort of safety. Grabbing a nearby length of broken branch, Gabriel struggled to his feet, hunching himself against the wind, and confirmed that he could move by leaning heavily on his improvised crutch.

Between savage gusts of windborne rain—or was it seawater, still?—he made his way forward, stopping to rest, stooped low against the wind when the storm threatened to sweep him entirely off his feet. Just after a particularly ferocious gust, his crutch struck a solid impediment of some sort, and he groped in the darkness, cursing the storm for failing to provide lightning now that he needed it.

Whatever laid in his path seemed to consist of rock and was perhaps knee-high. He made his way around the end of it, and sat heavily in the lee of the obstacle, relishing the relative quiet he found there.

For the space of several deep, shaky breaths, he sat, thanking the blessed Virgin for interceding in his moment of greatest need. It was in this moment, without warning, that a heavy piece of airborne debris struck him from behind, and he fell, senseless, to the ground.

Chapter 2

When Gabriel woke, the first thing he noticed was the starry sky overhead. In every direction beyond the patch of inky sky above, he could see flashes of lightning from the storm, but he was in some sort of strange islet of quiet air, enough to make him wonder if he were dead, and awaiting an invitation from San Pedro to enter through the gates of Heaven proper.

The throbbing pain of his head, answered with each beat of his heart by a matching throb in his leg, soon dissuaded him of this idea, however. He felt the back of his head, where he'd been struck, and found a lump there with a gash across it, but was reassured that the injury was not mortal. He sank back down into the muck where he'd fallen, and closed his eyes to compose a long and heartfelt prayer of thanks to San Antonio, the protector of lost sailors.

He barely noticed that he'd fallen asleep until the first fat drops of rain blew into his face. Opening his eyes, he felt the freshening breeze whip itself nearly instantaneously into a resurgent gale that seemed to be vindictively seeking out his shelter on this side of the obstacle that had, up to this point, shielded him.

A few more moments were all that it took to convince him that the wind had, indeed, changed direction. "*Dios mío,*" he muttered. Such a thing was outside of his experience—storms should blow foul out of one quarter only, not from every quarter of the wind! Painfully, he lifted himself up, relying on the comforting solidity of the barrier behind which he'd found safety, and moved around to the other side of it.

Debris was piled up on that side, affording him little in the way of the protection he'd enjoyed in the lee, but he shoved away a tangle of branches, heavy with mud, and pushed his way down below the height of the obstacle, even as a gout of warm rain poured over the crest, soaking him anew.

Some time into the endless succession of rain, wind and lightning that followed, Gabriel became aware that he was singing, finding comfort in the familiar melodies he had heard as a child, or the shanties of his fellow sailors, somewhat rougher in content and structure than what his mother sang to him in his youth.

He belted out the songs, unable even to hear himself above the storm, but keeping his attention off of the many indignities it continued to inflict upon him. Now sweeping out from the unseen land to his west, the wind was picking up all manner of debris, most of which passed overhead unnoted.

Some, however, dropped over the top of his sheltering barrier, covering him in a rough blanket of twigs, grass, and material he was just as glad to be unable to identify. Slowly, he noticed that the clouds were no longer lit solely by flashes of lightning, but that there was some sunlight filtering through.

Too, the wind no longer blew so hard that it threatened his ability to even draw breath. As the storm slowly abated, Gabriel began to sing improvised songs of thanks, nonsense, even babble, and he worried in some corner of his mind for his own sanity.

Eventually, the rain slowed to something less than a constant deluge, and though gusts still sometimes bent the trees that yet stood, he was able to rise gingerly on one leg from behind the wall where he'd spent the longest night of his life, and brush off the clinging coat that the storm had deposited on his form.

Through the misty sheets of rain that still fell, he could see a scene of utter devastation. The ship he'd glimpsed as he came ashore lay overturned in the distance, and he was shocked to realize that the wall he'd laid beside through the storm was what remained of a familiar landmark in town, the small mission where he'd celebrated his last Mass ashore before his fleet was to sail.

He recognized it only by the distinctive timber he'd noticed at the foundation beside the door when he had entered the prior Sunday. A single, massive oak bole, he'd wondered how any human team had been able to move it, and had been struck by the heartfelt, if crude, carvings of the Blessed Virgin along its outer edge.

He ran his fingers over the representation of Mary's smooth forehead, wondering at the power of the storm that had swept away every other remnant of the church, while sparing him more serious harm. He could see no other hint that there had been a structure of any sort on this site, much less the shacks that had clustered about the mission. Even more striking, it had easily been a mile from the church to where he'd clambered aboard the launch for the short row to his ship, and yet he'd been swept to nearly this spot by the waves. In the strange twilight of the dark storm clouds overhead, he could see the waves of the ocean still far inland from where the shore had been. He wondered idly when, if ever, it would retreat, while continuing to scan the land and sea for evidence that he was not the last living man on earth.

His makeshift crutch was long gone in the dark confusion of the night, but there was no lack of ready replacements available, and Gabriel began to make his way in the direction of the shore, hoping to find some sign of the rest of the fleet, or any other living soul.

The hurt leg had not improved any for the night in the storm. If anything, the throbbing was worse this morning, though his head, at least, only ached, rather than feeling as though it were in danger of exploding across the wrecked landscape. Gabriel tried putting weight on the leg, but the sickening pain this simple action brought on convinced him that he had broken at least one of the bones in his lower leg.

Once the wave of nausea from his experiment had passed, he looked around for a better walking stick than he had found close to hand by his shelter. A gnarled branch from a mangrove fit just about perfectly under his armpit, and a twist that had been rubbed smooth in contact with some long-gone obstacle formed a ready-made spot for his waterlogged and scraped hand to grab and hold.

Shaking his head to toss away the pain, Gabriel picked his way through piles of mixed debris. It looked as though every tree he could see had lost most of their branches, if they hadn't been snapped off at the base or knocked over, roots and all, forming great craters in the ground.

Everything was coated in a thick layer of muck, dragged up from the bottom of the bay and deposited to turn all visible into shades of murky grey. Through the mud, he could see heaps that might have been merely aggregations of plants, or could have been the corpses of animals—or even people.

Though the wind remained steady and rain came and went, the light was strong enough now that he could see for some distance around him. Little looked as though it were unscathed, though a few gulls screamed and cavorted in the winds in the direction of the bay.

Aside from the overturned hulk of the ship he'd already seen, there was nothing in evidence to hint that this had, at the prior dawn, been a busy, if small, settlement, or that a modest fleet had stood at anchor in the bay, ready for an expedition of war between his own King and the British sovereign.

He shook his head. Oh, how the mighty had been humbled, reminded that before God, all of Man's works were as playthings, and that those which did not serve His plans in any particular moment were forfeit to the power of nature He might unleash upon them.

Gabriel was overcome, for a moment, with humility at the fact that his own life had been spared, among the wholesale destruction that lay all about him. Falling to his knees, he spoke a fervent prayer to the saints, the Blessed Virgin, and the Holy Father of all, who had obviously chosen him for some purpose that was not furthered by his premature death.

As he struggled back to his feet and adjusted his mangrove crutch to bear his weight, he was startled to hear a voice behind him, the voice of a woman.

"*¡El muerto!*" she called. "How do you walk among us, though you have the look of the grave about you?"

Gabriel whirled about to see a woman with her hair streaming out over her shoulder in the wind, but otherwise appearing as though she had spent the storm in a dry and safe shelter somewhere. Her plain white dress and ebony hair relieved the uniform grey mud with a shock of color.

He looked down at himself, and could see at an instant why

she greeted him as the dead one—between the debris which clung to him, the filth of the bay that coated him, and the fact that his clothing was drenched to his skin, he supposed that he did look as though he were better suited for a grave than for a walk.

He walked toward her, noting that she bore a wary, suspicious expression on her face as he approached. "I was swept from my ship, and preserved from the storm by the grace of God alone," he answered.

"I will grant you that I was handled somewhat more roughly than you appear to have been," he added, gesturing with a wave of his hand at her appearance.

Her arms crossed before her, she regarded him for a moment, and then motioned with a toss of her head and a grimace, saying, "We weathered the storm in a cabin my father had insisted upon building into the ground, in the way he once saw in his travels. It is, for the most part, intact this morning, and all we who sought shelter there have survived."

She looked him over pointedly, and said, "You have found a more difficult manner of surviving the storm, it seems, but one cannot fail to be grateful for the blessings we are given, no matter how mixed they may be."

She dropped her crossed arms and held out her hand to him. "Come, let us see to your hurts, and hear your story."

He hobbled forward and she put her hand on his elbow, guiding him through the scattered rubble, back past the ruin of the mission. He tripped once and grunted in pain. She grimaced at him and, without any words, shifted over to the side of his injured leg and put his arm over her shoulder, taking his crutch out of his hand.

She moved to toss it away, but hesitated when he started to object, reaching for it, and she said, "Fine, I will carry it for you, but you will not need it at this moment."

He nodded and relaxed to let his weight settle across her sturdy shoulder. Though he was not accustomed to accepting assistance, he could not deny that they were able to move more efficiently across the smashed terrain this way. His stubborn pride was not so great as to prevent him from accepting the inevitable.

He also could not deny that her soft shoulder was a more pleasant way to keep weight off of his injured leg than the twisted branch, as fortuitously formed a crutch as that may have been.

"You wanted to know my story?" He snorted. "There is not much story to tell. I was on a ship, which was not a good place to be in a storm such as we experienced last night. I was hurt as I fell overboard, and I washed ashore."

He shrugged. "There is not much more than that to tell."

As they walked, the wind occasionally blowing rain into their faces, he noticed that she was peering about intently, and he asked, "Are you trying to find something lost in the storm?"

She pursed her lips and said tightly, "Not something. Someone. My husband."

Gabriel waited for her to explain, but she was finished talking about the subject, and the expression on her face made it clear that asking more questions would be both fruitless and unwelcome. She kept her stony gaze directed forward, her bearing discouraging him from making any further attempts at conversation, even to learn her name or family. In her turn, she seemed to have lost interest in hearing of his travails, and he regretted the sudden stop to their conversation.

He chose to put his attention instead to observing the caprices of the storm, noticing that some trees looked as though they had scarcely shed a branch, while others had been reduced to splinters. They crested a small rise, and he saw that it had given shelter from much of the wind, though there was still plenty of debris carried in from elsewhere.

Midway down the back of the hill, a low, solidly-constructed roof emerged from the ground, and the woman nodded in the direction of the structure.

"*Casa de desastre*," she said, her mouth quirking into a half-smile in spite of herself. "That's what I and the rest of the villagers called it when my father built it. We laughed at him then, but none are laughing this morning."

Gabriel nodded thoughtfully. "Your father is obviously a wise man," he ventured tentatively.

She wheeled on him, glaring. "My father is a fool in those things that matter. But for him, I would be walking together with my husband this morning, instead of dragging back a broken-down sailor."

She visibly regretted her words the instant they were uttered, as Gabriel drew himself up, balancing on his good leg and withdrawing his arm from her support, his expression a mask of anger and wounded pride.

Before he could speak, she blurted, "I did not mean that as it sounded. I am only—oh, it is too complicated." Her mouth again pursed, she shook her head angrily and blinked hard, looking away in denial of the tears that leaked out of the corners of her eyes.

They regarded each other for a long moment, unspoken anger thick in the air between them. She broke the quiet, saying softly, "I am sorry for my clumsy words. I am not angry with you, but with my father and my husband. They are both men of much *dignidad*, and with that sometimes comes much foolishness."

She gestured back toward the chaos that reigned behind them. "I fear that my Paulo has paid the price for their foolishness in this night. He argued with my father yesterday, and then refused to take shelter with us as a result of this petty fight. Today, I can find no trace of him, while you stand before me. It is not your doing, and yet I cannot help but feel your preservation as a rebuke to his foolishness."

Gabriel took a deep breath, his nostrils flaring slightly as he did so, and then nodded. "I have seen men permit their pride to drive them into grievous mistakes." With a slight relaxing of his face, he added, "I have even been guilty of such moments of pride myself."

He wobbled slightly as his balance on the good leg wavered, and he raised his arm back to the height of her shoulder. "If you can forgive me for being preserved through the storm, I can forgive you for being angry at me for doing so."

She nodded and moved back under his arm. He gratefully restored his balance with her support, and then said, "If I am to depend upon you, whether against my preference or not, I ought to know your name, shouldn't you think?"

She smiled at him slightly, looking up to see a quick answering smile flit across his lips. "I am Carlotta Dominguez Delgado. And you are called . . . ?"

He drew himself upright as far as he could, respectfully inclining his head in her direction. "I am Gabriel Llalandro Garcia y Cortez, and it is my honor to make your acquaintance. I only wish that I were in a position to offer you aid, rather than requiring aid of you."

She nodded graciously in reply, saying formally, "I am certain that when the day comes that you are able, you will offer any aid that I might need."

She gestured to the shelter, saying, "I will leave you with my father and our neighbors here, and continue looking for Paulo." He nodded, and they walked together, Gabriel steeling himself for the possibility that he would be witness to a continuance of the ongoing confrontation between Carlotta and her father.

He was surprised, therefore, when she opened the door and called out softly, "My father, this man needs our help."

He heard a rustling from within the shelter and out of the darkness stepped a short, stooped man with grizzled hair and a greying beard. Squinting in the comparative brightness of the overcast morning, he peered up at Gabriel's face.

"This is not your husband," he observed, his voice gravelly and firm.

"No, father, I must search further to find Paulo."

The older man sighed and nodded, closing his eyes in a sorrowful expression. "I still do not think it wise to venture out before the storm has spent itself completely, but then it is not my spouse who went out into it. I will take care of this man, while you search for yours."

He took Carlotta's place under Gabriel's arm and assisted the younger man into the darkness of the shelter, without so much as giving his daughter another glance. For her part, Carlotta turned and marched off into the increasing rainfall without any further comment, and without looking back.

Chapter 3

Gabriel woke with a start, taking a moment to remember how he had come to be in such unfamiliar surroundings. The air was dank with the smell of smoke, wet earth and the press of an uncomfortably large number of unwashed human beings in a close space for too long.

Though his eyes had adjusted to the darkness, he could see scarcely anything by the puny flicker of light given off by the small but functional fireplace at the back of the shelter. He lay where Carlotta's father had placed him, on a low, hard bed, too short for his injured leg, bound straight as it now was to a splint.

As he shifted uncomfortably, he found that he was not alone in the bunk. Another person—there was no way to tell who it was—lay beside him. Pressed against the rough-hewn log wall, Gabriel tried to move to relieve the pressure on his hip where he'd slept, and finally found a position where he could relax enough to perceive that his bunkmate was soundly sleeping, even snoring lightly.

Listening, he could hear only the sounds of people breathing, punctuated by the occasional pop or crackle from the fire. He tried closing his eyes and going back to sleep himself, but the ache of his leg was too great to permit him to relax sufficiently.

Too, his mind raced as he pondered the effects of the events of the past day. His ship's loss was but one small piece in a much larger setback resulting from the horrible storm. His had been one of a modest fleet of ships, mostly built for river travel, but pressed into service by Governor Gálvez in his plan to intervene on the behalf of the rebels against the British crown.

It had been a bold plan—sail swiftly upriver to Baton Rouge and seize the English post there, disrupting their plans to attack New Orleans. All swept aside now by the unpredictable power of the storm, a factor that he suspected was not doing as much harm to the plans of their enemies upriver.

He sighed inwardly. He didn't pretend to understand the motivations of kings or governors, and he resented it when their machinations interfered with his work as an honest sailor, recently advanced to the position of quartermaster. On the other hand, he reflected, the opportunities for extra profit as a smuggler did rise when faraway rulers squabbled, so it wasn't an unrelieved burden.

That was a risky path as well, though—the British had arrogantly posted a warship on Lake Pontchartrain, and Gabriel's ship had been stopped and subjected to search on several occasions. The British captain and his crew cared nothing for the proper stowage of cargo, and the additional work these searches imposed on Gabriel and his shipmates made trips upriver into chancy affairs.

Even in a small ship, though, there were always hidden corners—Gabriel's favorite had been a pocket of space just astern of one of the knee braces under the forward deck. A loosened plank readily concealed a sack or two of shot, and the American rebels were grateful to exchange some silver for the lead.

And then there were jobs like this one, where his captain had been persuaded by the governor to join the fleet. Gabriel did not know whether Captain Batista had been moved more by an appeal to his duty as a Spaniard or by the potential for plunder in the wake of a sacking of Baton Rouge, but in either case, Gabriel trusted the captain well enough to follow him into the fray.

Now, with his ship and many others lost, and Captain Batista's fate unknown, Gabriel could hardly guess what ships might remain for him to sign on with. He sighed again silently. From what he'd seen of the devastation without, there might not be any shipping left at all.

A rumble of thunder sounded outside, and he heard a fresh spatter of raindrops start on the roof, followed by the sound of another downpour beginning. Gabriel lost his train of thought in the soft rush of the rain, and sleep finally came to him.

Light from the opened door woke him, and around him he heard others stirring as well. The figure beside him rolled over, and he noted that it was Carlotta's father. The older man sat up and said, shortly, "There was no other place. The floor is too wet, and we have many who have taken shelter with us here."

He rose and went over to the fireplace, where two men and a young boy sat. He spoke quietly to them, and sat down with them. Glancing around the dark room, Gabriel spotted Carlotta, who stood up from a bunk on the other side of the crowded space. She met his eyes and walked over to him.

She sat down on the edge of his bunk, and he noticed that her eyes were red and her face puffy, as though she had been crying ever since the last time he had seen her. His expression formed the question that she answered with a slow, sad shake of her head.

"I found no sign of Paulo. When I found you, it gave me hope that he might have found shelter as you did." Punctuating her conclusion with a deep sigh, she said, "I must face the fact that I am a widow."

She closed her eyes and turned away, and Gabriel struggled upright to sit beside her. He sat quietly for a long moment, and then said, "Until you have buried him, you must not abandon hope." He waited until she turned back toward him, her eyes again bright with unshed tears, but with a shade of hope in her expression.

He smiled quickly at her. "Tell me about your husband."

She drew a deep, slow breath. "Paulo is . . . well, as I said, he is proud. Stubborn. He works as a farmer with my father, raising cattle. He is strong—I have seen him drag a full-grown bull to where he needed it—and he is very handsome." She looked down modestly at this, and Gabriel smiled.

"You have no children yet?"

"No, we have not yet been blessed with children, although we would both like very much to have them. We have been married only two years, and he has very often been away with my father."

Gabriel nodded encouragingly. "It is, perhaps, just as well that you do not have that worry at this moment, to add to your burdens."

She sighed deeply, replying, "I know you are right, but I cannot help but think that if I had given him children, perhaps he would not have been so quick to go out into the storm—"

With a gasp, she buried her hands in her face and jumped up, throwing herself back onto her bunk, where her shoulders shook with the unrelenting sobs of the bereaved. Gabriel wanted to offer her some comfort, but there was nothing in his power that could ease her pain and worry.

With a sigh, he pushed himself up off his bunk and hobbled over to where her father sat with the other men and the boy. Wordlessly, the older man moved aside to make room for Gabriel to sit with them.

"Excuse me, *señor*, but in the course of all that you did for me yesterday, I do not believe that we were properly introduced. I am Gabriel Llalandro Garcia y Cortez, a quartermaster of the river trade by profession, although—" he gestured ruefully at the door "—now without a ship."

The older man regarded him for a moment, and then answered, "Salvador Dominguez. I raised cattle, before they were all killed in this storm. I also know not what I will do now." He looked back down at the table, where he stared at his own hands for a long time before adding, "Whatever my daughter has told you about me, I am ten times as foolish, and ten times as wicked."

The older man stood, avoiding Gabriel's questioning gaze, and slowly made his way out into the daylight, his shoulders slumped and his head bowed.

Chapter 4

The sun was shining warmly, a light breeze flitted through Gabriel's hair, and he had become nearly insensate to the destruction all around him. Watching others working on cleaning up while he sat with his leg immobilized was nearly enough to drive him mad, but there was nothing to be done for it.

The men had organized themselves into a crew to clear ground near the shelter, and a number of them were ranging over the surrounding area, bringing back materials and what food they could salvage. They'd piled timbers as neatly as possible on one side of the cleared area, and someone had returned with a quantity of still-sound sailcloth they'd found in the rubble.

Two men were discussing how best to fashion a shelter with it, and Gabriel called out to them in a sudden burst of animation, "Let me see the cloth, and perhaps I can be of some assistance, despite my infirmity."

They brought it over and one man said to him, "We had forgotten that you are a sailor, and that you have experience with this material. Here, let us open it up, so that you may see what condition it is in."

Gabriel noted that it had the appearance of having been ripped from a relatively small ship while still furled—in places, rope was still wrapped around it tightly—and so was not surprised when the two men unrolled it to reveal a wholly intact jib, which formed a long, narrow triangle perhaps three paces across at the base, tapering to a point some nine paces away.

He nodded, saying to the man nearest him, "It's in good condition, and will serve to provide shade and some protection from rain as well, if it's rigged up well. It won't provide complete protection from the wet, but it will help. Have you found any loose rope, other than what was around it when you found it?"

"No, we hadn't yet found any, but I will send my son and his friend to look for anything that might serve." Gabriel nodded in reply, feeling for the first time since he'd gone over the railing on his ship that he might be able to help somebody else more than needing help for himself.

While they waited for the children to return with whatever rope they might be able to locate, Gabriel busied himself with undoing the line that had been wrapped around the furled sail to keep it wrapped. Simple for a sailor to untie, the knot at the clew cleat would have stymied any of the other men there, particularly in its waterlogged state, and would likely just have been sliced open, wasting valuable line.

He had the other men secure the clew and tack corners to the front of the shelter, pulling the length of the sail out away from the door, where he had them erect and secure a tall, stout pole while he directed them to secure the head end of the sail, once the boys returned with a shredded portion of what Gabriel judged to be the sheet line from a ship about the same size as his had been. He untangled it and parceled out the individual lines to the men who were now working under his direction.

When they were finished, the sail formed a long, narrow sunshade, tapering off to the point where it was attached to the pole. Gabriel nodded at it, satisfied. He'd spoken a few times over his career with sailors who had been shipwrecked, and they'd always praised the utility of sails for building shelters.

As Gabriel and his crew had been working on the shade, another group of men had hauled in a steer that had been killed in the storm. Gabriel turned away from the sight of the animal, which appeared to have drowned. He did not like the idea of eating anything that had been in the water like that and, like most sailors, had a particular horror of drowning.

He limped back under the newly built sunshade, smiling at the pair of boys who'd fetched back the rope as they scampered about under the shade, enjoying some game of their own devising. It amazed him how children could find entertainment in even the hardest times, but he supposed, too, that they needed to divert themselves from that which they could not understand.

After several minutes, he glanced back over to where the men had brought in the dead steer, and saw that they were already well engaged in the process of butchering the carcass. He could hear snatches of their conversation, and was gratified to hear that he was not alone in feeling reservations about eating a drowned cow.

A man holding a long, wickedly sharp knife was using surprisingly short, gentle strokes to separate the sodden skin from the corpse, carefully pulling it away from the tissue beneath as he cut. As he did so, he commented, "It still smells all right, so far."

"I don't know, Marcos," someone else commented. "I heard you say last week that you still smelled all right, and I know that wasn't true."

All of the men around the carcass laughed as Marcos fixed

the other man with an expression of mock indignation, pointing at him with the knife. "So you are saying that I had been too long out of the water, while this poor fellow was too long in it? Make up your mind, Fernando!"

Another round of laughter answered him, and he went back to the task at hand. Gabriel had to admit that the carcass looked much less unappetizing now that it was half-skinned, but he still felt much better when he looked away. He'd consider it further when it looked less like an unfortunate animal and more like meat in the larder.

As he averted his gaze from the butchering, Gabriel spotted Carlotta's father trudging over the lip of the hill into which his shelter was embedded. Slung over his shoulder was a dark form, the identity of which Gabriel was immediately certain he could guess.

He seized his crutch and hobbled as fast as he could to intercept Salvador's path. As he feared, the shape on the older man's shoulder was the corpse of a man. As he drew close enough to Salvador, Gabriel called out tentatively, "Paulo?"

The old man grunted and eased his burden down into the sodden earth at his feet. "No," he said brusquely, continuing, "but I dare to fear that I may yet find him as well."

Salvador rested for a moment, his hands on his thighs, bent over as though the man's weight were still on his shoulders. He took several deep breaths, looking at the face of the corpse before him. The man looked very young to Gabriel, and his face was composed, his eyes peacefully closed forever. There was no mark upon him, nothing to reveal how he had died.

"No, this is Julio, who worked for me also. I could not find him before the storm began, but now I have, and I need to go and confirm his wife's fear that she sleeps a widow tonight." Salvador straightened, a defeated look on his face, his posture bearing his weariness almost as a suit of armor.

Gabriel reached out and placed a hand on the older man's shoulder. "You have done much to preserve all of these people," he said, gesturing to the small crowd that was arrayed at their various tasks around the shelter. "None can fault you for the loss of a man whom you tried to save."

Salvador snorted, shrugging Gabriel's hand away angrily, and said, "And what of the man whom I chased out into the storm, to find his fate in the wind and the water? I have no doubt in my heart that my daughter faults me for his loss, and I agree in every particular. What good is it for me to save the village, but lose the one who was as a son to me?"

Gabriel could see the tears held tightly in check in the man's eyes as Salvador continued, "*Dios mío*, I wish that God would strike me down now, if only he would return Paulo to my Carlotta. I would gladly trade my life for his, and instead I traded his life for my pride. I have no right to call myself a savior of men with his loss on my conscience."

Gabriel responded quietly, "And as I have said to your daughter, until we have buried him in the ground beside Julio, we must not abandon hope. The Lord indeed moves in ways that are a mystery to us, and He may yet have a purpose for Paulo on this earth."

He sighed and nodded in the direction of the people still working around the shelter. "Now, which one is Julio's wife? Let us go and speak to her."

Salvador considered Gabriel for a moment, and then said, "I will go and speak with her alone. It is not your duty, nor your place." He grimaced. "I cannot attempt to give you a lesson about knowing one's place, but I assure you that this is more than you will be welcome to do."

The older man turned away and trudged down the hill, leaving Gabriel in Julio's silent company.

Chapter 5

Having gone to sleep to the sobs of Julio's widow, Gabriel awoke to shouts from outside the shelter. One of the boys rushed in through the door and ran up to Gabriel's bunk, saying in a rush, "There are men outside, and they are looking for you!"

Gabriel sat up as quickly as he could, grateful that he had awoken without the headache that had bedeviled him on and off since he was knocked out in the storm. Grabbing his crutch from beside the bed, he pushed himself to his feet and looked down at the boy. "Well, show me to them," he said, puzzlement and faint trepidation in his voice.

The boy scampered outside and pointed out past the fresh grave where Julio now rested, to a small group of men—on horseback, Gabriel was surprised to note. As he limped forward toward them, one of the men gave a glad cry. "Gabriel! We feared that you could not have survived. None other from the ship has been found, and yet when I asked at the last village whether they knew of any yet living closer to shore than they, they told me to try finding you in this place."

Gabriel blurted out, "¿Mí capitán?"

The man swung down from his horse, seizing Gabriel's hand enthusiastically. "Sí, I was ashore when the storm came in, conferring with the General about his plan for Baton Rouge. We were in a solid house in the city, and we were not so severely treated as were those closer to the sea." He waved a hand about at the heaped destruction still visible around them.

"Is the ship lost, then?" Gabriel knew already what the answer would be, but he needed to hear confirmation.

The captain nodded, his demeanor suddenly grave. "Indeed. All of the ships save one of the fleet are sunk, or smashed to kindling. We have received word that many of them are even to be found lodged in trees, rather than in their natural habitat afloat, and many good men were lost."

Gabriel nodded solemnly. "I have seen one such ship, as the storm raged. I have not been to the shore myself, as I broke my leg—" he gestured at the stiffly-splinted limb "—as I was lost from the ship, but I have heard nothing that gave me any hope for the fleet."

"There was nothing more to offer hope. It is a terrible blow to the General's plans, and places our position here in grave peril."

Gabriel looked sharply at the captain. "Are we under some threat, then?"

The captain nodded, his hand rising to cover his mouth thoughtfully. "It is not yet widely known, but once they received word that Spain has declared war on England, the British forces at Natchez and Pensacola began plotting to attack us in New Orleans. They've been resentful of the assistance that General Gálvez has been giving to the Americans."

The captain adopted a feigned expression of innocence, adding, "Just because we might have let quite a few of their supply ships slip through the British cordons on the river, and permitted them to trade openly in munitions, the British governor somehow got the idea that we have been favoring the rebellion since the General's appointment in New Orleans."

He held the expression for a moment, and then permitted it to dissolve into a smirk. "I suppose that there might have been something to that, after all."

Gabriel returned his smile and asked, "With the fleet lost then, what will the general do about these British plans?"

The captain leaned confidentially toward Gabriel and answered, "That is part of why he has sent me here. I wished to come to the shore regardless, but he is particularly interested in gathering these *isleños* to assemble a militia to go overland and surprise the British at their garrison at Baton Rouge. Do you suppose that they might be fit and willing?"

Gabriel pondered for a moment, and then replied, "Most of the men are fit; whether they are willing, I cannot say, as we have been bending all of our energies toward mere survival. I doubt that they will be glad to leave their families without proper food and shelter, though."

The captain waved dismissively. "Food we will have, and soon. The general has sent word to the *rancheros* in Texas to send cattle, and they can surely supply materials for rebuilding shelter as well. With those assurances, perhaps we can persuade some of these men to come to the aid of their King's service, eh?"

Gabriel nodded slowly. "I cannot speak for them, *Capitán*, but I believe that you may be able to raise a force from these survivors. Come, I will introduce you to them."

The captain gathered the other men in his party with a gesture of his eyes, and together the horsemen followed Gabriel's slow, limping progress back to the shelter, where they found places to picket their horses while Gabriel went inside.

Within the shelter, most of the people had awakened, and the women were busying themselves with preparations for cooking. Salvador was, as usual, sitting dourly at the table before the fireplace, not speaking to anyone, despite the hubbub of activity around him. Gabriel approached him.

"*Señor*, there are men outside who bring tidings from New Orleans, including the captain of my little ship, who has survived by the grace of God. I think that you and some of the other men will want to hear his news."

Salvador looked up at Gabriel, his expression inscrutable. Inhaling deeply through his nose, he said finally, "We may as well hear how they have fared in the city. David, Raul, Esteban, come, let us greet our visitors." The other men he had called to each rose and joined Gabriel and Salvador as they made their way to the door. Esteban looked at Gabriel, thoughtful and curious, while Raul and David were both somewhat less animated.

Blinking in the brightness of the morning, they emerged from dankness of the shelter, and Raul seemed to perk up at the clean, fresh breeze that was blowing in from the sea with the morning. All of the men stood up straighter and prouder than they had indoors, where the low ceiling forced all but the shortest into an uncomfortable stoop.

The visitors were engaged in a conversation amongst themselves until the captain spotted the men emerging from the shelter. He turned with the other visitors to greet the men of the settlement as they approached.

"Gentlemen, permit me to introduce myself. I am Manuel Batista Herrero y Covas, lately the captain of the ship on which my friend Gabriel served, and now representing Governor-General Gálvez. The general is saddened by the losses we have all suffered due to the terrible storm, and has asked me to assure you that he has arranged for assistance."

There was a grateful murmur among the men of the settlement, and the captain continued. "We know that you have raised cattle here, and I have seen with my own eyes the losses you have endured of your livestock. I will personally ensure that the cattle being sent here from Texas will replace some of your losses."

Salvador asked gruffly, "And what, *señor*, will you ask of us in return for this boon? We are not accustomed to the General's representatives bringing us gifts, no matter what our need may be. We have all made lives for ourselves here since we left the islands and, for the most part, we have done so without the General's care."

The captain replied, "When you left the islands, you were starving, as the trade in wine from your vineyards had failed. The general arranged for your transport and ensured that you would find land and the opportunity to rebuild your fortunes."

David nodded, speaking up. "It is true, *Capitán*, that the general did offer us the chance to make a fresh beginning in this place, but we are now once again left with practically nothing. From what will we re-build this time?"

"Have no worry," replied the captain. "The general will make certain that your families are provided for. At this moment, however, we face a serious threat, due to the plans of the British at Baton Rouge. You have heard, I am certain, that a state of war exists between our sovereign and the British King. The general has sent me here to call upon you to serve the King in the defense of

New Orleans from the fell designs of the English."

Raul spoke, his voice far softer and gentler than his fierce appearance would have caused one to expect. "Are you telling us that the English mean to strike against our settlements, as well as the capitol at New Orleans?"

The captain nodded vigorously. "Just so," he said. "The general has gotten intelligence that even now, they prepare their attack, and we have but days to disrupt this threat."

He looked around at the scattered branches, heaped debris and the makeshift shelter. "I know that this is not a time when you are looking to leave your families, and what homes you may have remaining, but your governor needs your service, and your settlement's security depends upon your action."

Salvador spoke again, his manner more accommodating than it had been. "Of course we will come to the service of our sovereign and our country," he said.

He nodded in Gabriel's direction, and spoke to the men of the settlement. "Our new friend is eager to serve as well, I am certain, but his injury leaves him unable. I am more comforted by his presence here, though, if we must be away for a time. My friend Gabriel, you will watch over our families, and see to their security until our return?"

Gabriel bowed his head, replying, "It would be my deep honor to attend to this duty, that you may serve our country."

Salvador turned back to the captain and said, "So then, it is settled. Can you spare a day with us to help us improve the shelter that we leave for our wives and children?"

The captain, in turn, bowed his head in respect, replying, "It would be our privilege to assist you in this, so that you may serve the general, free of worry for your families."

With the assistance of the captain and his men, the settlers finished clearing a new village square, and by sundown that evening, the outlines of a new settlement had taken shape outside the *casa de desastre*. There was still much to do, but a community cooking area helped to take the smoke and heat of the fireplace out of the shelter, and a large temporary shelter was well on the way to completion.

Before work had commenced, though, Carlotta had angrily marched up to where Salvador and Gabriel were discussing what needed to be done both before and after the men had gone north. She was accompanied by several of the other women of the settlement, all of whom looked as angry as she did.

"What is the meaning of this plan, leaving us here alone to put our lives back together? Are you determined to simply destroy us forever? What assurances has this *capitán* offered you as to when you will return, or whether you will return at all? What will we do after you are all pickings for the crows?"

As Gabriel stood uncomfortably beside him, Salvador held up his hands, waiting for her breath to run out so that he could get a word in to interrupt her stream of invective. "Carlotta, please, this is not a duty that we have sought out, but as it has fallen to us, we are obliged to answer the call of our sovereign and our nation. You know that as surely as you breathe, my precious daughter."

"As surely as I breathe? I know as surely as my Paulo no longer breathes that you have duties here as well," she cried out in reply, waving at the villagers with a gesture that Gabriel could not help but note was as graceful as it was impassioned.

Salvador reared back and inhaled as sharply as though she

had struck him and, for a moment, Gabriel had feared that he would respond in kind, but the older man had instead visibly controlled his response, and had let his breath out before replying in a soft, emotional voice.

"I know where my duties lie, Carlotta Dominguez Delgado. I must march away to battle in order to ensure that it never arrives here to threaten you. Do not assume that I have forgotten my duty to you, nor ever presume to inform me that I am failing to discharge them adequately. I pray to God for forgiveness for my mistakes, but it is not your place to answer in His name."

They stared at each other for a long moment, each with an expression that Gabriel could not interpret, but it was clear that their strong wills had clashed on many occasions previous, and that they would not easily resolve the latest hurts and guilts that had been laid upon them each by the events of the storm.

Finally, Salvador broke the silence. Turning to motion to Gabriel, he said, "I have been discussing with Gabriel what must be done to assure the comfort and safety of all who will stay. He has, by reason of his injury, volunteered to remain here with the rest of you."

She looked at him, a certain coldness in her gaze, and said crisply, "I would rather have had Paulo here," and then turned and marched away, followed by the rest of the women who'd borne witness to the argument. They appeared to be, variously, resolute in solidarity with Carlotta, as uncomfortable as Gabriel had been, or simply overcome with worry and sadness at the loneliness they saw before them.

However angry Carlotta may have been, she had efficiently organized the women, fashioning woven mats to use as roofing material for the time being. The hip-high grass along the dunes above the normal high-water mark were well-enough suited to the purpose, though they were still coated with mud, and nowhere near as versatile as the palm fronds that they were accustomed to using for temporary shelter in *las Islas Canarias*.

By the time the light of the late afternoon sun was slanting across the clearing, the men were lifting a framework of light timbers into place to hold the roofing mats, and the jib sail had been moved and positioned to shield the cooking area from both the damp and the heat of the day.

The women served everyone a meal of *ropa vieja*, or as close as they could manage with what peppers, onions and garlic they had hurriedly stored in the shelter before the storm had demolished their gardens. It was, perhaps, more heavily laden with meat than it might ordinarily have been, and it lacked some of the finer touches that they would like to have put into it, but there were no complaints as the shadows settled deeply around the clearing.

Sleeping under the stars for the first time since the dreadful night when he had awakened to the surreal pause in the storm, Gabriel laid himself down awkwardly on a sheaf of excess grass, nearby where the captain and his companions had laid out their bedrolls.

"I am indeed sorry that you cannot join us, Gabriel," the captain remarked as they both looked up at the deepening night.

"I am sorry as well, *Capitán*, but I will have my uses here, too, it seems. My leg will have time to heal while you are campaigning with the general, and it may be that by the time you have won the day, I may be ready to aid you in fitting out a new ship."

Manuel chuckled quietly. "You are an eternal optimist, my friend. We are to attack a garrison of British regulars, in a fortified position, using a volunteer force drawn from settlements that have just been lashed by a terrible storm. I should not say so, but I believe that the general acts out of desperation to bring surprise to the enemy, rather than waiting for him to strike at us whenever he sees fit."

Gabriel considered carefully before asking, "Will the very unlikelihood of this attack not take the British by surprise? If they are sitting behind their fortified walls, will they not be more relaxed about their watches, less disciplined in their movements, more prone to make mistakes when the crisis is upon them?"

The captain sighed, answering, "That is what the general is pinning his hopes upon, certainly. Once we have raised what ships we can of the fleet tomorrow, we will rejoin the general at New Orleans, and sail upriver to Manchac, where we will assault Fort Bute."

He sighed again. "If we can secure that, we will have but to continue to the fort at Baton Rouge, and, finally, Natchez, if we are to remove the threat that the British pose to our capitol, and deny them the ability to threaten the American states from the west." He chuckled again. "Are you still so optimistic that we will fit out a new ship together?"

Gabriel replied without any hesitation. "If the matter can be accomplished, I am convinced that the general is the man who can accomplish it. Are you sanguine to the chances that you will be able to raise some of the ships that were lost?"

Manuel replied, "My companions include Captain Fowler and his lieutenant, as well as the American Captain Pickles, who desires greatly to attempt the recovery of his crewmembers from the *Morris*, which carried away eleven of his sailors in the storm."

Fowler spoke up from where he lay, beyond the captain's bedroll, "The smaller boats, so long as their hulls are intact, we can pull out of the water with our horses. We'll dry them out, patch them up, and they're as good as new."

Gabriel called over to Fowler, "I wish you good fortune in your efforts, but I should be quite surprised if any vessel could have survived that storm without her seams and keels being cracked."

Speaking again to Manuel, he continued, "As for the men you take with you, I have not known them long enough, nor have I seen them under fire. However, Salvador is as resourceful a man as ever I have met, and the others I have met here are strong."

He nodded to himself in the darkness, continuing, "The general's soldiers with whom we worked as the general assembled the fleet were cunning and orderly. If they are typical of the regular forces he has at his command, he should not want for boldness from his army."

The captain answered as if he had seen Gabriel's nod, "It is not boldness that I worry for, but sheer numbers and capacity. The enemy has the high ground, the protected position, and likely has superior numbers as well. I do not believe that he knows that we expect him to sally forth to strike at New Orleans, but even absent that intelligence, he must anticipate that we may attempt our own strike."

With a sardonic cough of laughter, he added, "I expect, too, that he has our city under some observation, and is even now toasting the loss of the fleet to the storm."

Gabriel answered, "That may well be the case, but he

cannot anticipate such industry as Captain Fowler is prepared to exhibit. Will you be able to secure additional shipping, should the fleet prove to be entirely unrecoverable, or will you be forced to march overland?"

"Passing through the swamps along the river will impede us far too much to consider that course," he answered. "I believe that there will be sufficient boats to be found from further upriver, should that be necessary. The storm that ruined us here was likely spent by the time it passed Lake Pontchartrain. Though," he added with a rueful laugh, "we shall look quite the sports if we arrive at Baton Rouge and discover that the storm has already unmade the place on our behalf."

Gabriel laughed in reply. "It would deny the general the glory of a hard-fought victory, but permit the easy return of these good men to their homes. I should not reject such help from the heavenly Father, should he decide to offer it."

"Nor indeed will the general, should that turn out to be the case. My friend, we have much to do in the morning. We would do well to conserve our strength and get what sleep we can."

"As you order, *Capitán*," Gabriel replied. "Rest easy, and dream of glorious victory."

"And you, dream of quick healing. Sleep well, my friend."

Chapter 6

Gabriel sat in the afternoon sun, content and warmed by its rays. A coming shift in the weather was presaged by an ache in his leg, but he was well-enough satisfied with the way it had healed under Carlotta's close management. He could now walk with only the faintest of a limp, and had not failed to be as industrious as one man could be, with the eager assistance of a gaggle of boys.

The settlement, too, had recovered well from its destruction in the storm. A small cluster of homes now surrounded the village square, and while their construction was not, perhaps, as stout as the *casa de desastre*, the structures were nonetheless ready for any but the most violent of storms.

Gabriel had been able to muster a team of boys, just a bit too young to have joined their fathers in the militia, but capable enough of handling the heavy work while he healed. Together, they had methodically built one house after another, laying down walls of downed trees and adding roofs of saplings layered with woven mats held down with heavier timbers, yielding houses that were largely weatherproof.

The general had been as good as his word, and a small herd of new cattle were secured inside a pasture inland from the settlement, surrounded with cypress *pieux* fencing, each stake painstakingly split from the sodden cypress logs that the women had dragged to the settlement in teams.

It was awkward work to do before he could stand on his bad leg, but Gabriel had followed the detailed instructions offered by Yolande, whose husband had managed to save his splitting wedge from the storm. By carefully placing the sharp edge of the tool at the top of the log and hammering it into the grain with a chunk of heavy wood, he was able to start the stake splitting away.

Next, Yolande showed him how to alternate hammering and pulling this way and that at the handle of the wedge to control the split all the way to the far end of the stake. A couple of well-aimed blows at the end of the stake, and it was sharpened at one end to ease driving it into the ground.

He'd been able to catch up with the wood that the women had brought in before he could stand, and reached the point where he spent an hour or so each day working on another log or two, reducing it to a stack of stakes that some of the older children took and pounded into the ground to complete yet another segment of fencing, replacing the temporary rope boundary bit by bit.

Eventually, the near-daily excitement of rounding up cattle that had strayed through the rope had come to an end, as they'd completed enough of the fence to contain them entirely, with just a narrow gate still managed by rope.

Gabriel was surveying the fence with satisfaction when he heard a series of happy shouts from the direction of the shore. He stood and walked to the crest of the hill to see the women and children of the village streaming out to meet their husbands, fathers and brothers, cries of joy echoing over the landscape.

He hurried down the far side of the hill, joined by Carlotta, who was scanning the crowd for her father when she suddenly gave a great cry and ran ahead to greet a man Gabriel had not met before. She was sobbing incoherently on the man's neck when Gabriel reached them, and the man looked up from holding her, his own eyes streaming unabashedly.

He met Gabriel's questioning gaze and said over Carlotta's shoulder, "You must be Gabriel, of whom I have heard so much from Salvador. I am Paulo, Carlotta's husband."

When Gabriel recovered from his thunderstruck silence, he finally managed to stammer out, "It is an honor to meet you, *señor*, and an unanticipated pleasure. Your wife has told me much of you."

Paulo closed his eyes and stroked the back of Carlotta's head, a sorrowful expression on his face. He reopened them and replied, "I know that she thought me gone, but in fact, I had traveled up the river a bit when the storm overtook me. I was able to find shelter in a great tree, and when the storm had passed, I was certain that all that I had loved was simply gone."

His eyes filled with tears again and he pressed his wife's cheek to his chest. "I could not bear the thought of finding Carlotta cold and still, and so I fled inland, until I met some soldiers recruiting for the general's militia, and I joined them on the spot."

He shook his head, pursing his lips in self-recrimination. "You may imagine my surprise when I met Salvador as we were boarding a boat to sail up the river, and he recounted how desperately my wife had been searching for me. It was, of course, too late to come back, or even to send word that I was all right, and there was nothing to do but to see the campaign through to its end, and then come back home."

Carlotta, still overcome and beyond the power of speech,

clung to her husband as he said to Gabriel, "Of course, as we traveled, Salvador told me of your arrival here, and everything about you that he was acquainted with."

Paulo offered Gabriel his hand, concluding, "I thank you for consoling my wife in her grief, and for giving her hope by your survival." He looked Gabriel in the eye, adding, "I know from Salvador that you are a good and moral man, and I know my wife's grief. I am sure that your friendship and compassion have been a comfort to her. If you are ever in need, my house is truly your house."

Gabriel replied, "I could do nothing else, *señor*, and still wake up with myself in the morning. It has been an honor to be of assistance in your wife's time of need."

Just then, Gabriel heard someone shout his name from within the knot of people that had gathered around the returned men, and looked up to see his captain waving his hat. He bowed his head to Paulo and said, "Please, I beg your pardon, but I must speak with my former captain, who has also returned with your party."

Paulo bowed his head in reply, saying, "But of course. My wife and I have much to discuss, but I will speak with you at greater length later."

"I look forward to it, *señor*," Gabriel replied, and then turned and made his way over to where Manuel stood, beaming at him.

"Gabriel, my old friend. I see that you have already learned of one piece of the glad tidings that I bring. Let me acquaint you with the rest, if there is some place where we can sit and speak?"

"Of course, *mí capitán*, let us go and sit in the shade in the village square." Gabriel led the other man back over the hill and into the settlement, noting with pride the obvious degree to which the village's renewal surprised the captain.

"You have been busy doing more than merely healing your leg, my friend," he observed. "I should not have thought it possible for a man with such injuries to have achieved so much, but then, I should know by now that you are capable of greater things than those that most men would be satisfied by."

Gabriel nodded modestly, and led the captain to a bench beside the cooking area. "I have had a lot of help from the women and children of the village," he said. "They have been most industrious in restoring themselves to their prior state, and making such improvements as were possible along the way."

He waved away the captain's praise and said, "But enough about this—please tell me of the campaign from which you are returned."

The captain grinned broadly and said, "We have succeeded beyond all power of anticipation. The river is ours, and our allies the American rebels should have no more to fear from the British in their west. We have, indeed, enjoyed a glorious victory."

"When we spoke prior to your departure from this place, you were not sanguine at all about your prospects for survival, let alone success. What transpired to bring that about?"

"In addition to some good luck supplied in part by the enemy, we had the great good fortune to have been led by one of the world's foremost military strategists, my friend. General Gálvez outfoxed, outfought and outdid the British at every turn."

Manuel brought his hands together and with them, described a sinuous path, saying, "You know how the river twists and turns in the area of Baton Rouge, and roughly where Fort Bute lies, yes?"

Gabriel nodded, and Manuel continued, "When we reached Fort Bute, we found that the British had reduced its garrison to just a few dozens of men, who were perfectly glad to let us have the place if we would but suffer them to live." He laughed and said, "We were happy to make that arrangement, and so we won our first victory without so much as wasting any powder for it."

He continued, his eyes alight with remembered glee, "Once we occupied the fort, the general moved us to its north, so that the enemy would be unable to re-take it from our rear, and then we set off to Baton Rouge to set a proper siege of that place. Even as we marched on the city, though, Captain Pickles—you remember him, the American I introduced you to—fought a hot action on Lake Ponchartrain, and seized the British sloop there, despite being outgunned."

The captain closed his eyes and shook his head, a smile plastered across his face as he warmed to the story. "Captain Pickles demanded that the *West Florida* surrender, and the British captain laughed in his face. In the end, though, his laughter cost him his command, and his life. The *West Florida* now sails under the American flag as the *Gálveztown*, and the British are no longer harassing our shipping on the lake."

Gabriel flashed the captain a smile at this news, exclaiming, "It is high time that the trade on the lake was freed of the worry that the British might decide that it was smuggling. Not—" he winked at the captain "—that anyone we knew might have been smugglers."

The captain barked out a quick laugh, and then returned

to his story. "So, while this action was underway, the general had sent scouts up to Baton Rouge, and he learned from them that the British position there was strong and secure. But Gálvez, well, you know . . . he is a sly fox in battle, that one."

Rubbing his nose in relish, the captain said, "He sent a small detachment to draw the enemy's fire—and attention—to an innocent patch of woodland to one side of the fort, while he had the rest of us move the artillery in the night, right up to the walls of the fort. We were so close that we could trade musket volleys with the defenders, had that been our aim."

Gabriel raised his eyebrows in surprise. "Were you not well within range of their artillery, in turn?"

"Yes, but we had time to get our positions well dug in and fortified before the British could redirect their fire in our direction. We suffered not a single casualty, and when we opened fire on the walls of the fort, well—" he chuckled savagely "—there was hardly a pile of unhurt soil anywhere that our artillery could play. The commander of the British garrison there called for parley, and the general pressed his advantage right to the hilt."

"And why wouldn't he? He held the whip hand, from the sound of things," Gabriel replied.

"Indeed he did, and both he and the British commander knew it. When he emerged from the negotiations, not only was Baton Rouge ours, but he had forced the commander there to send word to Natchez that the British were to quit Fort Panmure there, again without us needing to even waste any shot on it."

He paused to chortle, adding, "Captain Pickles has finished the job, taking every British ship of account on the river and the lakes. The Mississippi River is in our hands, and we have wholly secured both New Orleans from the British, and the frontier of the American rebel colonies from a rear attack. It has been an utterly profitable couple of months, from every conceivable direction."

"What losses did we have? Any from this settlement?"

"All who volunteered here have been returned here, with the happy addition of our friend Paulo. In all, we lost but one dead and two wounded, while the enemy has buried some three dozen of their men, and another three hundred and seventy-five were taken captive."

"With many more such losses, the British will have no choice but to pack up their ships and return across the ocean," Gabriel exclaimed, continuing, perhaps a bit wistfully, "I only wish that I could have been there to aid in the victory, *mí capitán.* You return clothed in glory, while I have been dabbling in the mud with children. "

"Gabriel, you know as well as I that you have done essential work here, not least of which is to see to your recovery. Without you having recovered the strength of your leg, you could not now join the general in his next campaign."

Gabriel's expression, which had been edging into self-pity, now lit up as his eyebrows raised in an unspoken question.

Manuel laughed. "Yes, he already has plans to press his advantage, and so wise a man as you are can likely guess where he will next strike."

"With the Mississippi River and New Orleans itself secure, I should think that he would like to press to the east, and take Mobile. After that . . . " he trailed off.

"After that," the captain continued, "we shall let the General and the fates decide. For the moment, he is looking for volunteers for the spring campaign. You can sit secure through the end of the year, in New Orleans, if you like, or here, if you have unfinished business." Almost unconsciously, the captain's eyes flicked to where Carlotta and Paulo still stood, speaking with each other in low voices.

Gabriel followed the captain's gaze and flushed deeply. He gave the captain a poisonous look and said, "There is nothing between Carlotta and I beyond just friendship and gratitude. I have respected her mourning, and have argued with her constantly to keep an ember of hope alive—and I am no more than thrilled that her hope has been rewarded."

Manuel raised his hands, as if to shield himself from Gabriel's heated response. "I meant nothing of the sort, my friend. I know your character, and I know that you would never violate the vows of a married woman."

Gabriel pursed his lips, scarcely mollified. Within his own mind, though, he wondered just why he had reacted so strongly to his perception of what the captain's meaning had been. He considered, and then rejected outright the thought that he could have been entertaining thoughts about Carlotta. She was a friend and a hard worker, no more.

The captain waved his hand over the roofs of the settlement, just visible over the crest of the hill. "I meant only the work that you have been undertaking to help these people to restore their position prior to the storm. Are you satisfied that, with the return of the militia they can complete the work without you? Or would they profit by your knowledge and energy?"

As Gabriel pondered Manuel's question, the captain added, "I can offer you no more than a place to stay in New Orleans until we set off. Here, you have some purpose to keep you occupied and busy, which can only be to your benefit as you continue to get stronger and heal from your injuries."

He reached out and placed his hand on Gabriel's shoulder. "I will return to New Orleans to confer with the general in a couple of days. If you feel that you are no longer needed here, you can accompany me; otherwise, I will come for you in the spring, when we set off for the new campaign."

Gabriel nodded, his previous anger fading as quickly as it had flashed into being. "I shall give the matter some thought, and will do what seems to me to make the most sense."

"Of course," agreed Manuel. "Now, we must rally the men to unload the supplies we have seized from the British for the benefit of this settlement. They will be wanting to attend to their stomachs in short order, and I doubt that you are prepared to feed us all at this moment."

Gabriel quirked an eyebrow at Manuel. "Stealing food from the British, *mí capitán*? I should have thought that you would have better taste than that."

The captain shrugged broadly, a grin again spreading across his face. "Even the British use flour, Gabriel, and their weevils taste no different from ours."

He roared with laughter at the sour face Gabriel favored him with in reply, and the two rejoined the happy crowd of settlers to organize the unloading.

That night, as the insects and frogs called to one another in the darkness, Gabriel found sleep elusive. He'd had a long talk with Salvador as they labored together to unload the ship, and the older man had been in strange spirits.

There was something bothering him, but he was more taciturn than ever, answering only questions about the military action he'd been in—he had led the detachment that had distracted the British garrison at Baton Rouge—and even on that topic, most of his answers were but a word or two.

The moon was full and surrounded by only a few wispy clouds, casting nearly the light of full day onto the settlement. Gabriel gave up on sleep for the moment and rose to walk off his unease. Walking through the quiet settlement, he could hear an occasional quiet laugh of reunited husbands and wives, or the whimper of a child looking for his suckle, but for the most part, the settlers slept around him.

Following the path to the seashore, he gazed out at the small, flat-bottomed transport at anchor there. Its sails were furled, and in the still night air, the banner of Spain hung limply from the flagmast. Gabriel regarded the ship and found that his thoughts turned to Carlotta, whom he had met quite near the very spot where he stood.

What were his true feelings toward her? Might it be better for all concerned if he were to quit the settlement and return to New Orleans? He was not entirely comfortable with that thought, as he still felt an obligation to repay the unstinting kindnesses that the settlers had shown him in his convalescence, but if there were any chance that he was harboring an inappropriate interest in Carlotta, he thought it best that he remove himself from the situation.

He had just reached that dour conclusion when he heard a long shriek from the direction of the settlement, the sound of a woman's voice carrying over the dunes. It was a sound of anguish, and Gabriel ran headlong back to the village to discover its source.

Chapter 7

As Gabriel came over the top of the hill, the first thing he saw in the light of the full moon was Carlotta, standing in her nightdress as though she'd been turned to stone outside the structure where she made her home. She held her hands rigidly out in front of herself, dark in the half-light. As he approached, he could see that her face was streaked with tears.

She saw him, and gave a low moan that made him shudder down to his bones, a sound that would haunt him for as long as his memory preserved it. He could see now that her hands were stained crimson, and he could smell the sharp, metallic tang of fresh blood. He stepped up in front of her, his heart hammering in his chest, and though her eyes remained dull and unfocused, she moaned again.

In a quiet but urgent voice, his eyes fixed intently on hers, he asked, "What is the meaning of this, Carlotta?" Her gaze finally focused on him, and then she looked down at her hands and emitted a choked sob.

Gabriel ventured a hand on her shoulder, turning her to face him fully. "Carlotta, what is going on?"

Finally, she reacted to him in something approaching a conscious manner, turning to face her house and pointing toward it. As he looked at her extended finger, he saw a drop of blood gather and fall from her clenched fingers, and he wordlessly released her shoulder, putting himself between her and the house, and then approaching it warily.

Emerging from the shadows of the lintel, he could see the legs of a still figure, and, at an odd angle, a familiar piece of wood—the handle of the splitting wedge. The smell of blood was stronger here, and it was obvious to him that whoever lay before him was not going to be rising again in this life.

By this time, other members of the community had been roused and were gathering tentatively around Carlotta and her house. Someone lit a torch and brought it over to the house, and the scene revealed by the flickering light sickened Gabriel.

The figure in the doorway laid sprawled face-down, with the splitting wedge deeply embedded into the back of his head. A pool of blood was soaking into the dirt around him, and more was spattered on the frame of the door, running down the wood and leaving dark trails behind.

Gabriel turned away from the dead man, his gorge rising in his throat. Taking the torch from Marcos, who had carried it over and now stood dumbfounded at the sight it had revealed, Gabriel approached Carlotta.

"Who did this thing, Carlotta? Are we yet in danger?"

She shook her head violently, an expression of horror twisting her features as she sobbed almost silently. Behind them, Gabriel heard someone grunt, and then say in a hushed, almost reverent tone, "*Ay, dios mío.*"

He turned to see that Marcos had pulled the splitting wedge from the skull of the victim, and had turned the body over, revealing Salvador's blood-soaked face in the moonlight, his sightless eyes half-closed and his teeth drawn back in a grimace. Gabriel's stomach gave a lurch at the sight, and he turned quickly to avoid getting sick all over Carlotta. When he was done, he turned back to her, wiping his mouth with his sleeve.

"Who did this, Carlotta?" His voice was urgent and firm. She avoided his eyes, her face still contorted in anguish. "Carlotta. Look at me. Did you see who did this?"

When she continued to look away, he seized her chin in his hand and pulled her to face him. He saw in her eyes not the fierce intelligence of the woman whose friendship and counsel he valued, but an unreasoning animal fear, bordering nearby to outright madness.

He looked away from the sight, scanning the faces of the villagers arrayed about the two of them and the lurid corpse. Many of them now held torches, making it easy for him to see everyone who had gathered. Looking back at her, he shook her chin in his hand slightly to gain her attention and asked, "Where is Paulo, Carlotta? Did he kill your father?"

At that moment, Gabriel heard a disturbance in the crowd, and Manuel came bustling up, led by one of the young boys of the settlement. He shouldered his way through the crowd and as he reached the spot where Gabriel and Carlotta stood, he stopped dead to take in the sight of her chin gripped in his fingers, her hands soaked in blood, and her father lying dead behind them. Gabriel dropped his hand and Carlotta turned her head away again.

"*Santo Dios,*" Manuel breathed heavily when he recovered the power of speech. "Who would do such a brutal thing to a good man?"

Gabriel answered, "I do not know, *mí capitán*, but I am trying to learn what Carlotta has seen. Is Paulo anywhere to be found?"

The captain glanced over the crowd and answered, "I will find out if he has been seen." He hesitated, and then added, leaning close and speaking quietly enough that even Carlotta would not be able to hear, "I believe that there was some bad blood between Salvador and his son-in-law, beyond the disagreement that sent Paulo away from here in the storm. If Paulo cannot be found, I fear that she may have lost not only her father, but her husband as well."

He stepped away and looked at Carlotta's hands, murmuring, "*Qué horror.*" The captain shook his head sadly before walking off to search the settlement.

As Manuel walked away, Consuela approached and pressed a cloth into Carlotta's hands. "*Pobrecita,*" she murmured, wiping the blood from the stricken woman's hands.

Gabriel said quietly, "Thank you, Consuela," and took the cloth from her, taking over to gently clean Carlotta's hands. When he stopped, she glanced down and took a shuddering breath, and the expression in her eyes was less wild and desperate than before.

"I— I do not know who has done this," she whispered. "I . . . left to get some fresh water, for the morning. My father likes—" She broke off, closing her eyes and giving a small shake of her head, and then opened her eyes and continued, correcting herself "—liked . . . to have fresh water by his bed when he woke, to drink before he rose for the day."

She stopped, closing her eyes as fresh tears leaked from beneath their lashes. After several long, hard-fought breaths, she opened her eyes and forced herself to continue, "Paulo was speaking to him, but my father was in one of his moods all night. All he would say when I asked him about it was that he was tired from the militia service, but I could tell that there was something more . . . something bothering him, something that he was still fighting with."

She shook her head and took a great, deep breath. "When I returned, he was lying there and Paulo was nowhere to be seen." She looked down at her hands again. "I don't know how I got my hands . . . dirty," she said.

He glanced back at the body and noticed, in the brighter light of the settlers' many torches, an earthen jug lying on its side by the door, its contents spilled and mixed with the dead man's blood.

He turned back to the woman, who had followed his gaze, but had stopped at the sight of her father's corpse. "Carlotta?" She looked back to him, her eyes again wide and unreasoning in her face. "Carlotta," he repeated softly, putting his hand on her shoulder. "I still want to ask you some questions."

Slowly, she returned, and he nodded encouragingly to her. "Was there anything bothering Paulo? Did he seem to be himself?"

"He . . . he was happy to see me again . . . he said that nothing would take him from my side again, that he would keep me safe always, and never again lose faith . . ." Her tone became querulous and her voice rose to a wail ask she asked, "Oh, where is my husband?"

Gabriel pulled her into an embrace, comforting her as best he could as she wept into his shoulder. "I do not know, my friend. I truly do not know."

Manuel came back then, arriving in long, purposeful strides and Gabriel looked over the woman's shoulder with a questioning glance. "My friend, nobody has seen Paulo since we finished our meal, and I cannot say whether he has left this place. There are many tracks leading in and out of the village, and I have not seen him on any of them."

He glanced up at the full moon, now risen to stand nearly straight overhead. "If he has flown from this place, then he will be able to go far by this light, yet it is not bright enough to follow a man by."

Gabriel sighed, his hand gesturing helplessly behind Carlotta's back as she continued sobbing. "We do not yet know that Paulo has fled, nor should we assume that he has done this until we can speak with him. Let us address these questions in the morning."

He motioned Consuela to come back, and released Carlotta from his arms to her. "Consuela, please take Carlotta to rest while we attend to what is necessary here."

He sighed and shook his head. "*Mí capitán*, we must dig a grave."

Chapter 8

Father Lopez arrived in the early afternoon, having been urgently summoned to attend to Salvador's funeral. It was his first visit to the settlement since he had come out in the aftermath of the storm to bless Julio's grave and join the women and children in praying for the safety of the militia.

While they had weathered that trial, now the people of the village were, to a person, in a state of shock greater than any they had experienced since being resettled here from their beloved *islas*.

Salvador had shepherded them through the difficulties that they had suffered as their familiar, if tenuous, existence on *las islas* had come to a sudden end with the resettlement plan that Governor Gálvez had urged upon them. Salvador had reassured them as they learned the ways of raising cattle, a wholly new practice to most of them.

He had been an informal confessor, a guiding hand, offering advice and assistance as his fellow settlers struggled with both the ordinary and extraordinary challenges of constructing a new life together in a new place. Indeed, through his foresight and caution, they had been spared in the terrible storm that could have readily wiped them all entirely from the face of the earth.

In Salvador's brief absence in the militia, Gabriel had heard the settlers say a hundred times that they would defer this decision or that to his return, that they would ask Salvador how they should solve a given problem, that he would have the final word in a dispute.

And now, in a single stroke, all that was denied to them forever. Carlotta was shattered by her father's loss, Gabriel knew, but the rest of the settlement was crushed as well. As he greeted Lopez stepping off his launch onto the shore, he could even see the same sense of loss in the young priest's eyes.

The first thing Father Lopez said as he accepted Gabriel's hand was, "It is true, then? *Señor* Dominguez has been killed at the hand of another man?"

Gabriel answered solemnly, "I fear that it is true, *Padre*. He was attacked and slain in the night, and it is said that he had a quarrel with his son-in-law, who has not been seen since." He shook his head sadly. "This is a terrible event, and I fervently hope that you can bring some peace to the hearts of these people."

Lopez nodded slowly, frowning. "I know all too well how much *Señor* Dominguez meant to the people of this settlement. I only knew him for a short time, and he left an impression on me that will last until the very end of my days. He was a good man, flawed as all good men are, but with a heart of gold, and a godly demeanor. I grieve his loss severely."

He sighed. "As for *Señor* Delgado . . ." He sighed again. ". . . I wish I could say that it is a shock to me that Paulo may have committed such an act, but I have known him always to be a man with fire in his soul. He does what he believes is right, and rages against those who might stand in his way, or even question whether road he follows is the right one."

Gabriel answered carefully, "We have no proof of his guilt in this matter, only the circumstances that I have described to you."

"Of course," he said hastily, "we do not know for certain Paulo's guilt, but I will say only that I believe that he might be capable of such an act." He shook his head, in turn, and sighed yet again. "These are terrible times, my friend, and passions of all varieties are loosed upon us." Gabriel did not reply, but only motioned with his hand, leading Father Lopez up to the settlement.

The men of the village had reversed some of Gabriel's progress with the *pieux* fence, pulling up stakes and replacing them with rope barriers for the time being, so that they could use the flat boards to fashion a rude coffin for Salvador's body.

After she had comforted Carlotta, even rocking her in her arms to get her to go back to sleep, Consuela had taken a shovel from one of the men, and had dug up the stained soil at the entrance to Carlotta's house, dragging it away on an old cloak, and returning with clean soil to replace what she had taken away. She worked in complete silence, Carlotta slumbering within the house. The only sound was the chuff of her shovel driving into the dirt, and the soft thuds as she dropped it into place.

When she was done with that, the quiet, determined woman had wordlessly pushed her way through the cluster of villagers gathered in grief around Salvador's body, now lifted onto one of the tables in his *casa de desastre*. She'd finally spoken, calling for rags and water, and had slowly, methodically washed and dressed Salvador for his burial.

Now, as Father Lopez walked past the waiting coffin and ducked through the doorway into the dark shelter, he saw the old man's body peaceful in repose. Salvador's hands were clasped over his heart, and a clean cloth covered his face. Lopez crossed himself and spoke a brief prayer under his breath, taking a seat beside the corpse.

Gabriel, standing just outside of the shelter, bowed his head in respect for the dead man, and then went to check on the preparations for his burial. A solemn group of the men were just finishing shoveling the last bits of wet sand from the grave, which lay close by the still-fresh mound where Julio rested.

He nodded to them, and turned back to the village. As he did so, he saw one of the young boys running wildly up from the seashore, his eyes wide and fearful.

Running to meet the boy, Gabriel stopped him, putting his hand on the boy's shoulder and crouching before him. He met the boy's wide eyes with his own and asked, "What is the matter, Camilo?"

The boy answered breathlessly, "There is a man, *señor*, a man in the water. It looks like Paulo, and I was afraid to go any nearer to him, after what he did to *Señor* Dominguez."

Gabriel asked sharply, "He is in the water, Camilo? Is he swimming or floating?"

"He is floating, back and forth with the waves. I do not know if he is dead or just pretending, and I was too scared to go and check." His tone took on a note of pleading as he added, "You won't tell the other boys, will you, *señor*? They would laugh at me, I know, even though none of them would have gone near to him, either."

"Camilo, I will not tell them, but I need you to show me where you have seen this man."

The boy nodded and took his hand, leading him down the shoreline a short way, and then pointed at a dark form that Gabriel could see rolling loosely in the surf. He released the boy's hand and crouched beside him again. "Thank you, Camilo. Can you wait here while I go and check on him?"

The boy nodded, clearly struggling to contain his fear, and Gabriel gave him a pat on the shoulder. "I'll be right back." He straightened and walked down the sand to the shape in the waves.

As he drew closer, he could see that it was certainly a man's body. He continued forward and, as the surf splashed around his ankles, the corpse rolled over in an incoming wave to face toward him. It was Paulo, his features waterlogged and his eyes wide open in a glassy stare.

He was partly curled up, as though shielding himself from a blow, but Gabriel recognized his position as that of a man who has drowned, and he shuddered at the memory of his own brush with that fate. Gathering himself, he waded into the surf and seized Paulo's body under his arms, dragging him up onto the dry sand.

The body was still stiff with the man's struggle against death, and as Gabriel dragged it clear of the surf, he saw the skin of Paulo's foot tear and start to slip off over his heel. He dropped the body and, for a second time in as many days, turned away to retch, his hands on his knees to steady himself until he was through being sick.

Turning back to the body, he bent down and pushed Paulo's sightless eyes shut with his fingertips, crossed himself and said a silent prayer for the peace and salvation of the man's soul. Taking a deep breath, he turned back toward the settlement, angling toward where Camilo stood, craning to get a better look at Paulo's corpse. Ignoring the boy's rush of questions, he silently took Camilo's hand and trudged back to deliver the fatal news to Carlotta and the other villagers.

The grieving woman sat in her house with Father Lopez, where he was holding her hand and talking quietly to her. Her eyes were dry and puffy and her posture was listless, as though no further shock could reach her. Gabriel paused at the doorway and Lopez looked up at him, a questioning look on his face.

As he took in Gabriel's slumped shoulders and defeated appearance, he rose. "What has happened, *señor?*"

Gabriel motioned him outside, where Carlotta could not easily overhear and answered, "We have found Paulo. He has drowned, and lies on the beach on the other side of the dunes." Gabriel shook his head, still disbelieving the news he carried. "I know not how he came to drown, other than to guess that he may have misjudged the edge of the land in the night and slipped into the water."

Gabriel shuddered, adding, "I do not know what to tell Carlotta. She is now a widow, in addition to losing her father at the hands of a murderer."

Lopez looked Gabriel in the eyes, his expression searching. "Do you believe that Paulo was the murderer?"

Gabriel pursed his lips. "I still know not, *Padre.*" He shook his head in frustration. "We cannot now ask him about the events of the night, but the evidence that we have casts the most suspicion on him."

Father Lopez nodded. "We will bury them both today, but I will not suffer to have *Señor* Delgado buried in consecrated ground beside *Señor* Dominguez if I suspect that he was his father-in-law's murderer."

Gabriel nodded, closing his eyes in anticipation of the further pain that this would cause Carlotta. "I only wish that I could offer you some assurance that Paulo were innocent, and that he could be given a Christian burial."

"I know this, *señor*, but I cannot commend his soul to the Father if I am convinced that he has committed a mortal sin on this earth." The priest sighed deeply. "I will go and tell his widow that Paulo has been found."

Gabriel nodded, tears springing to his eyes. "I cannot fathom the sorrow that has been visited upon that poor woman," he said. "She has a strength of character beyond steel, but this may break even her."

Lopez nodded in reply. "She will need her friends close to her, señor. The women will wail together, and they will ensure that she is carried through this time, but your friendship is precious to her as well. She has told me of your service to this village in the absence of the militia, and she believes that you are as an angel sent from Heaven in their time of need."

Gabriel, taken aback, had to contain a snort of disbelief. "I am hardly an angel, *Padre*. I am but a sailor, and a man with faults and sins upon my soul."

"Of course you are, *señor*, but even men are sometimes sent by God to those who are in need. You are but a man, yes, but a good man, and you have preserved this settlement against the evil of these times. You must now do so again, to give these people some hope that their sacrifices and losses shall not have been in vain."

He put a hand on Gabriel's arm, steadying him. "You are equal to this new challenge, señor. I have seen the good in your soul already, in just these two sad visits I have made to this place. You told me before that you made a decision to live. I suggest to you that your survival had a purpose, and that the protection of these people may have been that purpose."

Gabriel said nothing, but nodded slowly, his lips pressed together and sadness in his eyes. "You may be right, *Padre*. I will keep your words in my heart as I decide where my duty lies next."

The priest bowed his head in answer and turned to re-enter the house, weariness emanating from his movements. Gabriel did not envy him his calling, particularly when his duties were as difficult as these.

Chapter 9

Gabriel stood beside Manuel at the back of the gathering, listening to the priest's solemn words as he completed the ceremony of committing Salvador's body to the earth. Both men were keenly aware of the disturbed soil in the distance, where Paulo's corpse had been hurriedly buried, with only the briefest of rites.

Carlotta stood at the front of the group, listening to Father Lopez recite the mass for the dead, and joining dully into the responses from the congregants. The phrases of Latin proceeded back and forth quietly and steadily, until the final "amen."

As the villagers lined up to each drop a handful of wet sand onto the improvised coffin, Carlotta completed this final duty to her father, and then slumped onto Consuela's shoulder to be led back to her house. Once everyone else had filed past, Marcos and Fernando, all traces of joy absent from their faces, bent to the hard labor of filling a second grave in the same day.

As they walked away from the graveyard to the feast of remembrance that the villagers had solemnly prepared, Manuel took Gabriel aside to speak quietly. "Gabriel, there is something that I feel I must tell you before I return to New Orleans with Father Lopez, though I will leave it to your judgment who else should hear it."

Gabriel, nearly past the ability to muster the strength for

more bad news, turned to Manuel and said wearily, "What is it, *mí capitán?*"

The captain grimaced in recognition of the burdens he was adding to Gabriel's shoulders, but continued, "Paulo and Salvador argued outside of my tent on the night after they discovered one another in the ranks of the militia. I had thought that it was not my place to say anything about it, but now . . ." He shrugged and continued, "Now, I think that someone should know."

Gabriel waited patiently for the captain to continue. Manuel took a deep breath and said, "Paulo had not merely concluded that Carlotta and the rest of the village had perished in the storm. He had in New Orleans taken up residence with a woman he had known in *las islas.*"

Gabriel did not gasp, but did draw a deep breath, distaste for both the story and the dead man's actions written on his face. "And how did Salvador learn of this?"

"He heard one of the men in Paulo's squad speaking to him of his *mujer ardiente*—his red-haired woman—back home, and since this is obviously not Carlotta, Salvador confronted him about it. Paulo confessed his infidelity, and begged Salvador's forgiveness, telling him that he was truly convinced that he was a widower, and that he sought comfort in the arms of a friend."

Gabriel made a sour face. "Paulo was doing this, while his wife was still carrying hope for his safety, and remaining entirely faithful to him."

Manuel nodded. "That was what Salvador said to him, as well as calling him names that I would not have believed an *isleño* of his generation to have uttered. He told Paulo that his duty was to return home and confess all to Carlotta at the first opportunity.

Paulo swore that he would do so, and I thought that would be the end of the sordid matter."

The captain grimaced and said, "I was wrong. During the bombardment of the fort at Baton Rouge, I saw something that I wish now I had acted upon, instead of trying to leave these two to settle their own affairs. Paulo and Salvador had returned with the militia from the mission to draw the enemy's fire into the woods on the other side of the fortification. They were assigned to keep shot and powder coming to the crews serving the mortars."

He made a mollifying gesture in advance of adding, "The general likes to give the militia jobs that require no close training or drill, so that they cannot do more harm than good if they blunder."

Gabriel nodded, answering, "It is only good sense, so long as he does so without offering insult to the bravery of the volunteers."

Manuel responded, "Yes, exactly. It is not a question of bravery, but only practice and training." He took a deep breath and continued his story. "In any event, the militia was to carry shot and powder to the mortars, as I said, and we had thrown up earthworks to protect our movements between the stores and the line."

He frowned, as though the rest of the story were distasteful to even recall. "Salvador was carrying a load of powder, enough for three rounds of mortar, and enough to utterly destroy both a man and his position, should they be set off prematurely. Paulo was returning from the line, and I saw him stop Salvador and direct him to a different path than had been laid out for their protection."

The captain's expression grew sourer yet. "I could see from

my position that it would have exposed Salvador to the enemy's musket fire, putting him at risk not only of being shot, but of setting off an explosion that would have brought our position to ruin. Fortunately, he ignored Paulo, following the orders that had been given him by his superior officer over the suggestions of a friend."

Gabriel's brows were raised in surprise and he said, "You believe that Paulo would have risked so much harm for the protection of his reputation?"

The captain shrugged and replied, "I can only tell you what I saw. When I confronted Paulo about it after the battle, he claimed that he was warning Salvador away from the route, and I accepted his explanation, but now, I believe that was an untruth.

"*Mí amigo*, I wanted to believe that Paulo was a good man who simply made an honest mistake. But after these terrible events, I cannot escape the conclusion that he was tormented by demons we cannot imagine, and that they drove him to acts we cannot comprehend."

He looked in the direction of Carlotta's house, to which the grieving woman had retreated, away from the feast in honor of her father's life. "I do not think that Carlotta needs to know of this, as it will only add to her burdens, at a time when she is suffering more than we can possibly understand. However, I think that Father Lopez made the correct decision in denying Paulo the dignity of a burial in grace."

"I agree, and I do not intend to make Carlotta's pain any more keen than it already is. To both lose her father and to bury her husband as his suspected murderer is a monstrous turn of events. To confirm those suspicions would be too much to ask any person to bear."

"I only sorrow that I ask you to bear them, Gabriel. It is necessary that somebody know, I think, but I wish that it did not have to be you, my friend."

With a heavy heart, Gabriel followed the captain back to the village, where the feast, such as it was, had already gotten underway. All day, he had heard the villagers saying, "If only the tomatoes had not been destroyed in the storm, we could have had *gazpacho*," or "without papaya, we cannot make my mother's *ensalada*."

However, with the addition of the captured British supplies that Captain Batista had brought down from New Orleans, they had managed to set out a full table of food, the biggest variety he'd seen since his impromptu arrival.

One cauldron, big enough to give a child a bath in, bubbled gently over banked coals, the tantalizing aroma of *cazuela de pescado* wafting up from it. Yolande had made the most of the vegetables she had secured from upriver, even before the captain's arrival, and had combined them with plenty of fish, making a rich casserole out of it.

Beef they had in quantity, thanks to the assistance arranged by General Gálvez, and several of the villagers had worked together through the day to make a large number of *empañadillas*, plain British flour transformed into fried pastry surrounding spiced meat, and arranged them on an enormous platter on the table beside the *cazuela*.

Another cauldron was full to the brim with the now-familiar *ropa vieja*, the steam rising from the surface carrying its peppery smell upward to Gabriel's nose. As the British supplies had been unloaded, young Luisa had practically shrieked with joy and had seized the box of peppers Manuel had brought. Today, as she ladled out the stew, she was far more somber, but still clearly proud of the dish.

More of the precious flour and some hoarded spices had gone into loaf after loaf of *pan de las palmas*, their sweet smell perfuming the air. Despite the sadness of the day, and the additional weight on his soul from the intelligence that the captain had shared with him, Gabriel found his mouth watering and his spirits rising.

He greeted each of the villagers quietly, taking some of the food each offered, and then sat by himself, as there was nobody left in the village with whom he felt close enough to share the sadness of his mood, save Carlotta, and she was not in evidence. He supposed that Consuela had brought her back to grieve in private in her house, but did not even feel that it was his place to inquire after her.

The other settlers ate in small groups, speaking quietly among themselves. From time to time, he would overhear a story of a happier time being shared and see someone smile at a memory of Salvador, but for the most part, everyone seemed to be still struggling with the knowledge that they would have to complete re-building their village without the benefit of his energy or wisdom.

Gabriel looked over at the *casa de desastre*, marveling at the foresight it demonstrated. Peering more closely, he saw movement in the shadows inside, and stood to go and investigate. Still chewing a mouthful of bread, he walked over to the entrance, his eyes taking a moment to adjust to the darkness within.

Like a specter, he saw Carlotta slowly walking around the inside of the shelter, touching everything as she passed. Her face was composed and calm, past feeling any emotion at all, and she moved silently, almost as if her feet were not even touching the ground.

She turned toward him and gazed right through him, as though he were completely invisible, continuing her tactile examination of the table, the fireplace, the tools and the bunks. Her fingers trailed almost longingly over everything as she walked past, and as she drew nearer, he could hear her singing quietly to herself. "*Duerme, duerme, pobrecita. Duerme, duerme, Mí chiquita* . . ."

She trailed off and looked up at him suddenly, as though seeing him for the first time in her life. Confused, she asked him, "You are . . . you can hear me?"

Gabriel nodded silently, standing still in the doorway. Carlotta slowly bobbed her head, thinking about this information for a long moment, and turning back to touch the rough tabletop where her father's corpse had laid.

She looked up again and said softly, even dreamily, "My father built everything in here."

Gabriel replied, "I know that." He paused, considering, and then ventured to add, "He was a brilliant man, and he will be keenly missed by everyone here."

She looked at him quizzically, her head tilted in an unspoken question, and then nodded again. "Yes. Yes, we will all miss him a great deal." Her restless hand came to a stop on the frame of a bunk and she added, "But he will come back with Paulo soon, once they have finished fighting the British at Baton Rouge. Gabriel told me to expect them back any day now, and so I must ensure that the *casa* is in good order for them."

She smiled shyly at him and continued, "My Paulo will be jealous, of course. Gabriel is a good man, a much gentler man than he is, and I don't mind telling you—you can keep a secret, can't you?—that he is a very handsome young man, too."

Gabriel held his breath, aware now that Carlotta was not in her right mind. He knew that her spirit was wandering now between this life and one that would never happen, and he feared what might come to pass once she returned to find that the world that was real was so different from the one she now inhabited.

Her face now bore a puzzled look, as she said, "Gabriel...yes, a very kind man, he helped me so much when my father had his accident. I . . . I spilled my father's water . . . He will be so cross when he wakes and there is nothing for him to drink."

She looked at Gabriel, her expression gently pleading. "Won't you help me find another pitcher to get water for my father? He will need water so much when he wakes. He is very badly hurt . . . " She looked down at her hands, and gave a small start. "There is so much blood . . . he's hurt, won't you help me?"

She rushed toward Gabriel, stopping suddenly just in front of him, holding her hands before her just as she had when they had dripped with her father's blood. Her eyes were again animal with fear and hurt and confusion, and he reached toward her, freezing as she began to speak in a jumble of words, her voice high and quavering.

"Won't you help me, Gabriel? He's hurt, and I cannot find Paulo, but I know that he is hurt, too, he wouldn't have hurt my father, but they are both so cold, so cold, so still, so cold and so much blood, and I need to fetch more water for father, he will be very thirsty and quite cross when he wakes and finds that I have spilled his water all over the blood and when I tell him that Paulo has gone as well, and—"

She swayed and Gabriel caught her as she fell, easing her to the ground, kneeling to cradle her on his lap as he wept for her, for Salvador, for the village, even for Paulo. She lay mercifully unconscious for many minutes, and he still held her tenderly, tears coursing down his face, when Consuela found them.

She silently lifted Carlotta's arm over her shoulder, raising her to a standing position. Gabriel stood, too, and without a word, wrapped Carlotta's other arm over his shoulder. She seemed to return to a state of semi consciousness as they got her to her feet, and together, they walked her back to her own house.

After they had laid Carlotta down in her bed, Consuela had arranged the poor woman's legs on the bed and covered her with a thin blanket. Gabriel turned to leave, and she reached out suddenly, stopping him. She stroked the side of his face with her withered hand and said, in barely more than a whisper, "She is lucky to have you here. Thank you for your help. We are all lucky to have you here, my child."

Gabriel walked out into the sun, the bright daylight dazzling his eyes, and met the questioning looks that the villagers gave him with a steady, if red-eyed gaze. Manuel caught his eye and frowned, worry written clearly in his expression.

Gabriel turned away from the villagers and walked to the house where he'd been living and entered, lying down in his own bed to attempt to escape the demons that now stalked this place.

He slept fitfully, aware of activity outside the house as the villagers continued the honor their dead, eating and drinking, talking and even still laughing from time to time. At one point, he thought he heard Salvador's gravelly voice, and he sat bolt upright.

The dead man stood at the base of his bed, blood trickling

down his face. "Gabriel. You know your place here, do you not?"

Gabriel nodded, speechless. He could not help but think that it was probably impolite to stare at the wound on the old man's head, but he could not tear his eyes away from it. "You have done much already for my friends, Gabriel, and I know that you have your own path to follow. It will take you from this place soon enough, and that is as it should be."

The old man closed his sightless eyes for a moment, and then looked again at Gabriel. "While you are still in the village, I would ask a favor of you, if you will grant an old man the patience to listen for a moment?" Gabriel nodded again, still transfixed by a fresh rivulet of crimson that trickled unnoticed across Salvador's cheek.

"I ask only this of you, Gabriel: make sure that Carlotta is well before you leave her here. She is stronger than even she knows, but you must remind her of that, just for a little while. Will you do this for me, my friend?"

Gabriel tore his eyes away from the drop of blood that hung now on the point of the old man's jaw and nodded once more. "I will take care of her for you, Salvador. You may rest in peace, and know that your daughter is in good hands."

Salvador nodded in reply, dislodging the drop of blood, which fell onto his collar. The old man looked down at it and smiled at Gabriel. "It doesn't hurt, my son. Not one bit. *Vaya con dios*, Gabriel."

Gabriel said automatically in reply, "*Vaya con dios*, Salvador."

Salvador smiled broadly, perhaps for the first time since Gabriel had met him, his eyes crinkling in a deep set of laugh lines that Gabriel had never before noticed. "I do believe I shall, Gabriel. I do believe I shall."

He turned and walked through the door, disappearing into the blinding sunlight outside.

Chapter 10

G abriel awoke with a start, fully dressed as he had been when he collapsed onto the bed. At the door, in the light of the late afternoon, he could see Camilo staring quizzically at him.

The boy asked, "Are you feeling better, *señor?*"

Gabriel sat up, swinging his feet to the floor. "Yes, Camilo, I am rested, and I do hope that I have not given the others cause for worry."

Camilo slipped into the room fully and sat beside Gabriel, without waiting for invitation, dangling his feet over the edge of the bed. The boy looked up at him, his expression frank. "Some of them are worried about you, but most of them save their worry for Carlotta."

Gabriel stood up, nodding. "As well they should. I share their worry at this time. Has she risen yet?"

The boy shook his head. "No, Consuela won't let me get near her. She gives me the evil eye and even fetched her broom one time. So I came to see you instead." He hopped down beside Gabriel. "Let's go and see if she'll let you see Carlotta."

Gabriel gave the boy a crooked smile. "No, let's leave her in peace. Consuela is right; she needs as much rest as she wants right now."

The boy pleaded with Gabriel, "Please can we go and see?

Nobody will do anything but talk about her until she comes out, and I can't eat any more, and I'm bored because everybody is too worried to play."

In spite of himself, Gabriel laughed and started to follow the eager boy out of the house. Somehow, he felt more sure of his place in the community than he had before these tragedies had struck. It was then that he remembered the earlier visit from Salvador, and he stopped dead in his tracks.

"What is it, *señor?*"

Gabriel held up his hand to shush the boy and stood for a moment, frowning into the gloom of the house. Shaking his head, as if to send the strange vision away, he lowered his hand and answered, "It is nothing important, Camilo. Just recalling a conversation with Salvador and, I think, making sense of what he was telling me. Let us go and speak with Consuela."

At the entrance to Carlotta's house, Consuela greeted them quietly, her eyes glittering darkly at Camilo, though she forbore to scold him.

She said to Gabriel, "She still sleeps, but she no longer tosses and turns in her torment. At one point she cried out, and then spoke in her sleep, though I could not understand what she said. It was as if she were conversing with someone, but there was nobody there."

Apparently exhausted from such a lengthy speech, Consuela shrugged and said no more.

Gabriel asked, after a moment, "May I go in and see her?"

The old woman nodded in answer and stepped out of the threshold to let him pass. As Camilo moved to follow Gabriel into the house, her arm shot out and blocked the boy's way. He scowled up at her and she scowled right back at him, shaking her head disapprovingly.

Gabriel entered the room, his eyes adjusting to the low light within. Carlotta lay sprawled out on her back, her open palm hanging over the side of the bedframe. Her head was thrown back and her mouth slightly ajar. As he stood there, he could hear her gently snore.

He crouched beside her bed and gazed at her for a long time, listening to her breathe and thinking about his encounter with the deceased Salvador. He could see her father's heritage in the shape of her nose and the set of her brow, and though her hair was at present unkempt, he remembered with a smile how like an angel of mercy she had looked with it blowing in the storm's wind when he first saw her.

She looked peaceful now, and he wondered what he could possibly do to help her feel as serene when she awoke. He shook his head to himself and stood. Although he did not yet understand how it was his place to aid her, he felt in his heart that Salvador's charge to him must be respected.

Looking back at Carlotta's placid form one more time, he went back outside, still shaking his head. As he emerged, Consuela seized his elbow, fixing him with a piercing look. "You can help her," the old woman said. "It is what Salvador wants." She released his arm and stepped back into the shadows. A chill ran down his spine as he realized what she had said, but before he had a chance to reflect deeply on her words, Camilo was at his side.

"How is she doing? Will she die, too? How did she look?"

Giving the boy an exasperated look, Gabriel answered, "She

will be all right, in time. It takes more than a day to recover from the loss and shock that she has had."

He looked down at the eager boy, remembering what Camilo had seen on the shore. "Well, it takes most people longer than a day to recover from a shock like that."

The boy ignored his comment and led him out into the common area where a few of the villagers still sat in conversation with Captain Batista. Gabriel walked over to his friend and waited until David and Esteban's conversation with him had trailed to an end.

The two villagers gave him almost identical nervous little smiles, David grasping Gabriel briefly on the shoulder as he passed, and they moved on to leave him alone with the captain. Gabriel greeted him. "Manuel, I thank you for your help through these difficult days."

"My friend, it is my honor to offer my service to you in these matters. Are you feeling better than you were after the feast?"

Gabriel nodded. "I am much rejuvenated for having gotten some sleep, and further comforted to see that Carlotta is resting as well."

Manuel gave Gabriel a friendly but calculating look. "You will remain here until we sail for Mobile, then?"

Gabriel nodded. "I have even greater duties here now than I did when you arrived. Salvador's murder leaves these people without a natural leader, until Carlotta regains herself." He frowned thoughtfully. "I believe that they will do as she directs them, and that they will profit by her counsel, but at the moment, she is out of her mind with her loss."

"Of course, Gabriel. I understand that you feel a certain

responsibility for the fate of this settlement, where you were saved and permitted time to recuperate from your injuries. Of course, now that Paulo is gone, and not just missing, have you considered what your intentions toward Carlotta might be?"

He raised his hands, stopping Gabriel's exclamation before he could even give it voice. "I know, it is too soon to discuss it, but I must sail with the tide tomorrow, and so there will not be any other time to speak of these matters, man to man."

Gabriel pursed his lips before answering, "You seem bent on involving me with this poor widow, but I neither know whether she would want to be involved with a sailor, nor whether any intrigue that I might develop in that pursuit would be in her best interest."

He tossed his head, as if angry at a thought that had entered it. "You have me doing it again, Manuel. I am worrying again about what is best for her, and though Salvador wishes that I should see to her care, I do not know whether there is anything that I can truly do to take care of her."

Manuel's eyes widened slightly. "Salvador wishes you to see to her, Gabriel?"

Gabriel briefly explained the visit he had experienced after Carlotta's collapse and his own. Manuel listened without comment, wincing as he described Salvador's wound. When Gabriel had finished his story, Manuel nodded.

"I have little doubt but that Salvador was greeted by *San Pedro* at the gate, and was welcomed in to meet the Holy Father without delay. And as for you, you have been given this task directly by Salvador as his final wish. I well understand that you cannot do anything but follow his instructions to you, and I wish you only the happiest of fortune as you discharge this duty to Carlotta and her father."

"Thank you, *mí capitán*, for not ridiculing me with disbelief of what I saw, and thank you for your blessing as I do as I must for the people of this settlement."

Manuel shrugged. "I cannot say that you were not visited this day by Salvador's spirit. I hope that should I have so urgent a task to complete as seeing to the safety and care of a daughter, that I should be granted the time and ability to do so, whether before or after I sleep in my grave."

He clapped Gabriel on the shoulder. "I must go and get some rest before we are to slip our anchors tomorrow. We will have a busy time of it in the morning, so let us say our farewells now. May God be with you as you comfort and protect Carlotta. I know that you will do all that is right, and that these people will benefit from your presence among them."

"I will look for you at the end of the year, *mí capitán*, and will pray for the success of our plans at that time." Gabriel hugged the man in a moment of deep gratitude and watched as he walked over the dune to return to his ship for the night.

The next morning, Carlotta was not in her bed when Consuela went to check on her, and the old woman rushed into Gabriel's house to wake him. "*Señor*, come quickly," she said urgently into his ear. "Carlotta has gone in the night."

He sat up, bleary-eyed. The night had been filled with strange and terrible dreams, and to wake to find the day beginning with such bad tidings left him feeling as though he'd never slept at all. He blinked hard to clear his eyes and regain his focus, and asked Consuela, "Where?"

"I do not know, but I do not think that she will have gone

far. Her shoes still sit beside her bed, and I thought that Salvador would want to trust you to find her."

Gabriel shot the old woman a quick look, but she was looking out through the doorway with deep concern, while her hands worried at the rosary beads around her neck. He sighed and lifted himself out of the bed. The emotions of the past day had left him feeling as though he had been engaged in heavy physical labor, and his joints ached nearly as deeply as his heart.

He stood blinking in the sunlight for a moment, thinking, and then strode toward the shelter on a hunch. He was unsurprised to find Carlotta there again, but this time she had a cleaning rag in her hand, and was busily putting everything within into order.

At the sight of her, barefoot and still wearing nothing more than her nightgown, Consuela gasped and rushed ahead, pulling her own shawl off to put around the younger woman's shoulders. "Come, child, you must not wander about unclothed," she scolded, but Carlotta did not seem to be aware that she was even present.

She straightened the benches on either side the table, bending to carefully wipe the seats. As she did so, the shawl slipped from one of her shoulders and hung over her awkwardly, unnoticed. Gabriel stepped inside, ducking to avoid cracking his head on the low ceiling timbers, and quietly said her name. She glanced up, nodded to him, and turned to lift one of the bedding mats, flipping it over and smoothing it with sweeping motions of her hand.

"Carlotta," he repeated, stepping forward again, this time taking her arm gently.

She shook his hand away and continued to smooth the mat with her hand. She said, "I do not wish for anyone to call this place *'casa de desastre'* ever again. That name was a disrespectful way of reminding my father that I blamed him for Paulo's absence, which he never deserved. I never knew how much it wounded him each time I called it that, or convinced someone else to do so."

Straightening, she looked at him and continued, "In honor of my father, we shall name it 'casa de Salvador,' for not only was it his idea, but it also was our salvation. It will be kept as he kept it, in readiness always, for any disaster that may befall us. This is as he wishes."

Pulling the shawl back over her shoulder, she called out, "Consuela, I thank you for the mantle, and I will come and dress as soon as I have finished what I am working on here."

Noting the expression of concern on the old woman's face, she continued, "I am feeling much better today now that I understand what my father sacrificed for us, what he hoped for us. I was so consumed with my anger at him that I could scarcely recognize how much he loved us all, and how great was his commitment to our safety."

She turned to Gabriel. "I know that you understand when I say that I want to be alone in this place for a little while. I can feel my father's presence here, and I wish to spend just a little more time with him, before I have to return to the world that rejected him."

Gabriel looked at her for a moment, examining her eyes and seeing no hint of yesterday's madness in them. Finally, he nodded. "Consuela and I will be waiting for you, Carlotta. Salvador's primary concern was your well-being, and we have both been given the charge of ensuring that."

She looked at him steadily and replied, "Yes, I know, and I will allow you to look after me once I am finished in here." She waved at the shelves around the fireplace. "I have only a small amount of cleaning yet to do."

Bowing his head, Gabriel turned and left the shelter, joining Consuela outdoors in the morning air. He placed his hand on her shoulder and said, quietly, "I think we can leave her for the moment."

She hissed at him, "What new madness is this?"

He shook his head, a thoughtful look in his eye. "I do not know if it is madness, or, if it is, I think that you and I may share in it."

She gave him a narrow, questioning look, and he responded, "I know what I saw yesterday, and I think you do as well. Is it not to be expected that his daughter saw the same, and that it gave her some peace and new strength?"

The old woman crossed her arms and cocked her head to one side as she considered this. Slowly, she nodded. "Salvador is still looking after what is best for his daughter," she said.

Gabriel agreed, "Yes, and I think that he has helped her to find what is best for her in this moment. Caring for his legacy to the settlement offers her not only a way to guarantee that legacy, but also to share in something that was important to him."

He got a distant look in his eyes, and said, more to himself than to Consuela, "I think, perhaps, that is something that we all seek when we think of our fathers."

She favored him with a rare—and brief—smile, saying, "Or when we think of our mothers." She sighed quickly and rubbed the side of her neck, as though acknowledging for the first time the pains of the morning. "I think you are right, and that this is doing her no harm, and may indeed be giving her some peace."

With an impatient gesture, she concluded, "I just wish that

the girl would put on some clothes."

Following old woman back toward the houses, Gabriel glanced back inside the shelter and smiled quickly to himself. He did not doubt that Carlotta was more comfortable dressed as she was, no matter what disquiet it caused Consuela. As for himself, he was satisfied that her clothing covered her modesty, and beyond that, he was not concerned with what meaning a particular garment might have.

After eating a breakfast of cold *cazuela de pesca* and *pan de las palmas*, Gabriel watched, with a heavy heart, as Captain Batista ordered the sails of the schooner shaken out to catch the morning breeze upriver. While he knew that he had responsibilities here in the settlement, he burned to be onboard, attending to his duties there.

The little ship tacked back and forth and hove out of sight, Manuel waving his hat from his place at the tiller, and Gabriel waved in reply until his friend had rounded the bend. He stood and looked at the empty river for a long time before returning to his house.

Later that morning, Carlotta walked past his place on her way back to her own, and he stepped out into the light to greet her. He noted that her eyes were puffy again, betraying the fact that she had again been crying, but she was calm and collected.

He asked, "The shelter is returned to its original state?"

She nodded and brushed a stray lock of hair out of her face. "Perhaps even better than my father was able to maintain it. I have closed the door against the next time that we might need it, and would be grateful to you if you could give out the word that I wish it to be undisturbed."

She frowned, adding, "I do not wish it to be used as a charnel house again, in any event."

Gabriel nodded, a pained look crossing his face at the memory. "They knew not what else to do with your father, Carlotta. Do not be too swift to judge them in their confusion and hurt."

She tossed her head dismissively. "I know that they did not have a better place to put him, but I mean both that I do not hope to see any others laid out, and that I do not wish to see the shelter used for distaff purposes again."

"I could not agree more wholeheartedly, Carlotta. We need all our strength for the trying times to come, I am certain."

She looked sharply at him. "You mean to leave again, don't you?"

He sighed. "I have my duty, Carlotta, and our country is at war. I had no choice about staying here for the campaign at Baton Rouge, but I cannot remain in safety here while the men of your village are fighting."

She gasped, her face pale. "You mean to draw away our brothers and husbands a second time? It is not enough for the governor to have brought us to this place, far from all we knew and loved on *las islas*, not enough to take them up the river to face the guns of the enemies, not enough that they return so full of rages and demons that they kill—" She broke off and ran for her house, sobbing uncontrollably.

Gabriel sighed and went back inside. He wished that he could change the arrangement of the world for her, and tell her that she had nothing to fear, but it was beyond his power.

Chapter 11

L ife in the village settled into a comfortable routine for several weeks afterward. Working together, the settlers slowly rebuilt the homes and the other elements of the village that had been lost in the storm, including the mission building. It took nearly all of the men to drag the enormous oaken foundation log from its old location, closer to the bay, over the rise and to where the new settlement had been laid out.

They positioned it carefully, though, and built a small, comfortable sanctuary around it again, which Raul insisted on referring to as their "*catedral*," to the amusement of those who'd worked on it, and to the particular annoyance of Consuela.

Generally, though, the men were more solicitous of their wives than usual, more appreciative of the comforts of home, and aware that their duties would likely soon call them away again. Mealtimes continued to be a community affair, as everyone had come to enjoy gathering around the cooking area in the middle of the new village.

Today's dinner was a crawfish stew, using crawfish that Camilo and his friends had gathered. He'd wheedled Consuela into giving him some liver from a calf that had broken its leg in a hole, and had called the other children over by a swampy spot along the river for lessons on how to catch crawfish.

He pinched off a bit of the liver with his fingers, pulling a face for the benefit of Elicia, who giggled obligingly. "Now you just tie it up with a string," he explained while he knotted a loop around the liver.

"And then . . ." he said, dropping the liver into the water at the edge of the swamp, ". . . you wait for a crawfish to come and take a bite." He'd picked his spot well, and within moments, a crawfish almost half the size of his hand could be seen scuttling out from under the bank to investigate the liver.

He watched intently, gauging the perfect moment, and then yanked the string up, with the crawfish's pincer clamped tightly to it. With a practiced movement, he swung the creature over to his other hand, and clamped his fingers around its middle. The crawfish indignantly released the liver, now waving its pincers around to try to pinch Camilo's fingers, but the boy grinned and thrust it into a sack, which he then spun closed.

"See? Easy as can be," he said. "Who wants to try first?" His friend Ernesto pushed his way forward eagerly, and Camilo handed the string over to him. As Ernesto dropped the liver into the water, the other children watched intently. Camilo absently pinched off and tied up a second piece of liver, which he handed to Elicia with a shy smile.

Moments later, Ernesto gave a triumphant shout and yanked his string out of the water, a second crawfish swinging from it. This one was either cannier or luckier than its companion, though, and slipped off the bait, splashing back down into the water. Camilo patted his friend on the back and said, "Don't worry, you'll get it next time."

Just then, Elicia gave a tiny shriek, and they turned to see a crawfish fastened to her finger. "Get it off me, get it off me, get it off me," Elicia shouted to Camilo, shaking her hand violently before his face.

"Hold still, then," he said, grinning, and grabbed her wrist and, in short order, the crawfish, which he was able to give a little squeeze to encourage it to release her finger. That one joined the first in the sack, and then he turned back to examine Elicia's finger.

"You'll be fine—it didn't break the skin." Then, embarrassed to be holding her hand, he released it and joked, "I guess you didn't taste good." She replied by sticking her tongue out at him and he laughed.

By then, Camilo had successfully secured his first catch of the day, and the other children wanted help getting their own bait set up. The morning passed happily, punctuated by the occasional yelp as a crawfish got the better of one of the children.

By noontime, Camilo and Ernesto, both grinning widely, presented Yolande with two large sacks full of the wiggling crustaceans. She dumped each sack into her cauldron full of boiling water, shaking it to dislodge the stragglers clinging to the sides. The boys watched, fascinated, as the creatures' shells transformed almost instantly from mottled brown to bright red.

They were turning to leave when Yolande called after them, "You boys stay right here and help me shell these things." They reluctantly returned to watch her carefully pour the water out of the cauldron, the steam fragrant with the salty, earthy smell of the cooked crawfish.

Waving the steam away, she pulled one out and tossed it from one hand to the other until it had cooled enough to handle. She quickly snapped the tail back, separating it from the front section, and tossed the head into a pot full of fresh water.

She then split the tail down the belly side with her thumbs, hissing through her teeth at the heat of the shell on her fingers. She pulled the meat out of the tail section and threw the shell in with the head, dropping the meat into a large pan.

"All right, now you try," she said, reaching through the steam to grab a crawfish for each of the boys. They were nowhere as efficient as Yolande was, but it wasn't long before they were nearly keeping pace with her. Between the three of them, the pot of cooked crawfish was quickly reduced to a pan full of tail meat and a pot full of rich-smelling crawfish stock.

She shooed the boys off, pretending not to notice that Ernesto had secreted a pair of crimson claws with which to menace the other children, and continued preparing the stew, humming to herself. By the time the men had wrapped up their construction work for the day, the stew was ready to be ladled out into their bowls.

Although they were weary from a long day of re-clearing the path to the bay, Gabriel and Marcos were joking easily back and forth about the rotting hulk that still sat, perched in the shattered boughs of a cluster of live oak.

"After we finish the road, you want us to pull that ship out of the trees for you, Gabriel? Then you can have your own command, eh?"

Gabriel laughed, "I have not yet found a ship worthy of my command, and a hulk full of holes is hardly fit for a man as skilled as I am on the river, in any event."

Marcos roared with laughter, replying, "Well, it may be that it is unworthy of you, my friend, but perhaps you can mend its broken ribs as well as you have your broken leg?"

"It is a hopeless wreck," Gabriel said, shaking his head and smiling. "Believe me, I have examined it closely. I believe that it is a boat that I had seen in port before I joined Captain Batista's crew, and it was hardly in any better condition afloat than it is now."

Marcos raised an eyebrow at Gabriel, saying, "Then how is it that it survived to the trees, while Captain Batista's ship was lost to the ocean?"

Gabriel frowned slightly at this gibe, and then shrugged, smiling and shaking off the stab of regret that he felt for the loss of his ship. "It may well be that the crew managed to sail it to safety once they were rid of me, and that they are now enjoying a happy cruise of the Gulf of Mexico, without a care in the world."

Then he sighed, adding, "Sadly, Marcos, you are right; my ship lies on the bottom of the bay, and only the blessed Virgin knows how many of my crew rest in the ocean with it." On that somber note, he stood, nodding to Marcos, and walked over to where Carlotta stood speaking with Consuela.

He could see from a distance that they were engaged in an animated discussion. As he approached, though, Carlotta saw him coming and shook her head quickly to Consuela, motioning with her chin in his direction, and both women fell silent.

He did not dwell on this, though, and bowed his head in greeting to them, saying, "I hope that you are happy, Carlotta, with the progress we have made today?"

She regarded him silently for a moment, and then, pursing her lips, shook her head. "Am I to rejoice at your work on readying the very road that will take your militia away to war?"

Gabriel sighed inwardly. It always came back to this question, and they had each rehearsed the arguments back and forth, over and over again. "You know that I wish it were otherwise, Carlotta, but I have bent all of my efforts to ensuring that you will be safe and comfortable in our absence. I know not what else I can do to satisfy you."

Wary of being drawn yet again into their ongoing argument, Consuela quietly stole away, leaving Gabriel and Carlotta facing each other, alone.

She tossed her head impatiently. "You and your captain can leave me and this place and these people in peace, and forbear to draw us into a war that is not ours to fight. Do you not think that we have suffered and lost enough?"

He snapped, "Neither Captain Batista nor I are drawing your neighbors into anything that they are not willing to do, Carlotta. We are, all of us, bound by our commitments to our sovereign to rise in response to any military need he may find for us. This is not a matter of simple blood lust, nor is it due to some desire to leave you here."

More calmly, Gabriel placed his hand over his chest to emphasize his sincerity, saying, "It is a matter of our honor and our duties as subjects of King Carlos of Bourbon, in Madrid. He has decided that we must go to war with the British, for whatever gain he perceives for our nation's position; we cannot question his command. He says to fight in his name, and we can do no other."

Still she scowled at Gabriel, answering, "The King is not living in a hut far from his real home, counting his blessings for every potato that some far-off benefactor deigns to send him. I did not want to come to this place, but my father, may his soul be at blessed rest, believed Governor Gálvez when he told us that this place was like a paradise on earth, and persuaded us all to accept the governor's offer to relocate us here."

She waved a dismissive hand at the settlement around her. "You ask whether our progress here satisfies me, without ever asking me once whether the goal you work toward is anything that I want. Perhaps I was not interested in re-building these shacks, and waiting for the next storm to blow them into splinters. Perhaps I did not desire to wait here with the other women and the children, not knowing whether those we love will return from the King's adventures. Perhaps I wanted instead to return to *las islas* and to the life that I knew before all of this happened."

She stopped spitting her arguments at Gabriel and stood, arms crossed over her chest, glaring at him furiously. He could see that her eyes were bright with tears of anger and frustration, but there was nothing he could offer in the way of comfort or an adequate answer. He, and the men of the militia with him, were trapped between the duties of fathers and brothers and the duties of subjects of His Royal Highness, the King of Spain and the Spanish Indies, a wise and brave conqueror himself.

Gabriel sighed. "Carlotta, were it in my power, I would sail you back to *las islas* myself, and build you whatever home as would make you feel happy and secure in that place or in this. However, I have only those powers granted to me as a human being, and strain as I might to be greater than my birth, there are yet limits."

He looked her in the eyes, holding her gaze firmly, and asked, "What is there within my power to do for you that would make you hate me less for being a party to those things that are outside of my power?"

She continued frowning at him, and finally sighed, uncrossed her arms and shrugged. "There is nothing you can do, Gabriel.

You did not bring us here, nor did you have any hand in our King's decision to enter the war and the governor's decision to ask us here to serve in his militia."

She sighed again, her shoulders dropping as she looked wistfully into the distance. She said more quietly, "I suppose that I am angry with you because everything was different before you arrived. I was a wife and a daughter, a respected member of my community, and I knew my place in building a future that was better than the past had been."

She turned away from Gabriel, her voice dropping nearly to a whisper. "Now I have none of these things, and everyone looks at me with either pity or blame in their eyes."

Turning back to him, she asked, "Do you see, then, why I might be angry with you, though I know that you have no part in my suffering? Even as you are recovering your place in your world, I have lost every part of my life that meant anything to me. As you have been healing, my hurt has gotten deeper with each passing day."

He stood looking at her, helpless, as she began to weep again. "I have not known how to rise out of bed each morning for a month, and once I do awaken, I know not why I continue to breathe, while the two men I respected and loved above all others lie in the cold earth."

She looked up at him, her eyes pleading, and cried, "I do not know how I am to survive, Gabriel, and you are a reminder that yet more loss awaits. I suppose it should come as no wonder that I am angry at the sight of you, filled with despair at the thought of you, and that I cannot wait until the day that you are in my past, and my future is less filled with doubt and fear."

He bowed his head, affected by her torment, and when he looked up, his eyes, too, were filled with tears. "I am not without sympathy for your position, Carlotta, and I fervently wish that I could do more than give you my assurance that I will strive to my utmost to ensure that no more sorrow visits you. These are dangerous times, however, and I cannot make you any such promise."

He held his hands out in a gesture of what seemed almost like supplication and said, "I hope that you will, in time, find it in your heart to forgive me for being your personal storm crow. Like that unhappy bird, I do not bring the tempest, yet you cannot help but feel dismay to see me if you believe that I herald its arrival."

His chin dropped to his chest again, and he stood there, silent, until he felt her hand brush against his cheek. When he looked up, she was favoring him with a wan smile. "You are not my personal storm crow, Gabriel, nor do I truly blame you for the sadness I have known since you entered my life."

She sighed deeply and added, "Send them back, Gabriel. When my friends and neighbors have done their duty to our King and country, send them home to us, intact, and I will never again fear to see your arrival."

He bowed his head, and then looked back up at her, saying, "I shall do whatever I can to bring this to pass, Carlotta. It may not be within my power, but I will bend my every effort to this task. It is the least service that I can justify doing for you, after your many kindnesses and services you have rendered to me."

She nodded at him and said, "I can ask no more of you." She gave him a veiled look and added, "I already know in my heart that you are a man who can keep such promises, if they can be kept at all."

Looking past him, she said with a sigh, "We have chosen a fortuitous time to have this conversation, it appears. A fleet sails even now down the river."

Gabriel whirled, and saw the masts of many ships just visible over the rise beyond the village, gliding smoothly downriver. By morning, he knew from experience, they would clear the mouth of the channel, entering the Gulf of Mexico, and turn to anchor in the bay.

He turned back to Carlotta and said earnestly, "I will keep my word to you, Carlotta, and I shall hope to return here as your friend when I have done so."

To his surprise, she rushed forward and threw her arms around him, hissing fiercely into his ear as he recovered enough to return her embrace, "You had better, Gabriel Llalandro Garcia y Covas. I shall accept nothing less."

She released him and turned, marching away with her head held high. Gabriel noticed that the villagers within view all seemed to be suddenly very busy and looking elsewhere. He shook his head rapidly to clear his muddled thoughts and went back to his house to gather his few belongings for the voyage ahead.

Chapter 12

Gabriel awoke, shouting, to the familiar shriek of wind through the rigging, and the tossing, skittering motion of his ship in a storm. His heart fluttered in his chest like a separate living creature trying to find a way free of the cage of his ribs, and his brow was soaked in ice-cold sweat.

Although the rational kernel of his mind assured him that this ship was more than able to manage the storm, the animal portion of him was certain that watery death strode upon the decks above. He lay, petrified, and listened for the signs of an unfolding disaster above decks.

It was evident that the wind and waves were catching the ship from an awkward quarter, accounting for the crabbed motion he could feel, but he did not hear the sounds of falling spars or blocks, nor the wrenching flap of sails being carried away. There was comforting purpose to the ship's movement through the waves, and knew that the master was in control, despite the rough water they were in at the moment.

He was, in any event, grateful beyond measure that he was not needed above until the morning watch, by which time he hoped that the storm would have blown itself out. Reassuring himself and taking slow, measured breaths to quiet his heart, he listened to the creak of the ship's timbers and did his best to let the sway of his hammock lull him back to sleep.

Listening closely, he could sense that the sound of the wind was relatively regular, and soon enough, the master had swung the ship about so that its motion was less chaotic, riding up the crest of each wave and back down into the trough beyond in a controlled, if unsettling rise and fall of several ships' lengths for each wave.

At each crest, the ship would either slowly tip forward to slide down the face of the wave, or, if its momentum were sufficient, burst through the face of the wave to fall freely for a moment before landing on the downward slope. The former was conducive to settled sleep; the latter was most definitely not. After a series of waves that left Gabriel and his surroundings momentarily weightless, and then dropped all back to earth's inviolate gravity, he gave up utterly on rest, and focused his thoughts on anything that might distract him from his current distress.

Against his volition, he found that his mind wandered to something even more distressing than the wild motion of a ship in high seas—the enigma that was Carlotta. As expected, the fleet had anchored for a few days in the bay, and Gálvez had again called upon the men of the settlement to serve in the expedition to Mobile and Fort Charlotte.

Carlotta had avoided Gabriel as the men gathered up the necessities, said their farewells, and formed up to march to the ships. Just as they were ready to leave, though, she had rushed out, her hair unbound and streaming behind her in the breeze, and had presented Gabriel with a small dagger in an elaborate, finely-worked leather scabbard.

"It was my father's," she explained breathlessly. "I am giving it to you, not as a gift, but as a loan, against your need for it to fulfill your promise to me. I know that you will return it to me without fail, and that will ensure that you are as good as your word, but also that you will come back to me yourself."

Gabriel had placed his hand on his breast, so moved was he by her entrusting this heirloom of her father's to him. "I will do as you command, Carlotta, and I will look forward eagerly to the day when I can return this boon unharmed, and, with the blessing of the Virgin Mary, unused."

She had nodded, seemed about to say something more, and then left nearly as quickly as she'd arrived. Gabriel could think of nothing else to do but to order the militia into motion, toward the ship that would take them away to war.

The fleet had departed under fine weather, and had been joined in a couple of days by an American ship, under the command of the same Captain Pickles with whom Gabriel had been acquainted so many months before.

Looking ahead to where Manuel waited for his shipmate, Gabriel could see the raised eyebrow, but did not volunteer an answer when he approached his friend. Without a word, the captain turned and fell into step ahead of the men of the village, leading them up the gangplanks stretched to the shore from where their ship lay at anchor.

The dagger now lay tucked away safely in Gabriel's makeshift sea-chest, and he fervently hoped that he would never find himself in so desperate a situation that it would turn the tide for him. From time to time, though, he took it out and gazed at the blade, noting the minor nicks and scratches along its edge, and wondering what tales the cold steel might tell, were it able.

Each time he handled it, he found comfort in its weight in his hand, and eventually, he simply threaded it into his belt, and he felt as though Salvador—and Carlotta—walked with him while he wore it, so it became a part of his daily uniform.

Manuel did not have his own command in this fleet, but had left Gabriel and the villagers on their ship to go and serve alongside Gálvez on the flagship. He'd said to Gabriel before they departed, "With luck, we will capture a prize or two along the way, and I will again sail my own ship, but for the moment, I am content to serve the great man in this capacity."

"I wish you the greatest fortune possible, and rich prizes enough to go around for all in the squadron who desire them," Gabriel had said. In his own heart, he might have wished for a small command, but for the heavy responsibility that already rested upon him.

Thinking about those responsibilities, he almost chuckled to himself at the thought of the villagers in this storm. Where he was merely unable to sleep, he knew that they would be, to a man, stricken by the *mal de mer* that affected those whose stomachs had not fully adjusted to the rigors of an environment where nothing was stable, and nothing stayed in its place—not even the floor beneath your feet.

They had all spent time at the railing even when the ship sailed in the light seas of the open Gulf, and the first time that they had been in a light chop, even while Gabriel cheerily walked along the deck chewing a piece from the last of the bread that had come with them from New Orleans, they had again lined the railings. Many of them had cursed at him for his immunity to the malady that gripped them, but he had only smiled, confident that they, too, would eventually develop the stomach for sea travel.

Nothing could prepare a man's gut for this sort of abuse,

though—many experienced sailors would be feeding the fish tonight. Gabriel, though, was one of the fortunate few who seemed truly to have a complete immunity to weaknesses of the stomach, and as the master found a smoother course through the waves, he was even able to slip back into the cool embrace of sleep.

When he again awoke, this time to the bosun's whistle, he was gratified to hear that he'd been right—the storm had abated, and the seas had calmed considerably. The wind was still stiff, but now steadily blowing from a favorable quarter for their journey.

Coming aboveboard, though, he saw with dismay that the deck, which had been crowded with barrels and crates of foodstuffs, powder and shot, was swept nearly clear. Here and there, forlorn scraps of rope that had been used to lash the supplies in place lay torn apart by the waves of the night, and Gabriel's heart sank.

He'd known that there was little choice about storing the supplies on deck, with the need to house an invasion force of men belowdecks, but this sort of disaster could well doom the entire expedition. Without food or arms, there was little that they could actually do at Fort Charlotte beyond harmlessly taunting the defenders.

With any luck, the other ships of the fleet would have had better luck with their stowage, and Gabriel looked now out at the ocean, to see how they might appear to be situated. It was then that he noticed that the captain of their ship was high aloft in the rigging with his telescope, and everyone was keeping a weather eye on the horizons. The rest of the fleet was nowhere to be seen.

Chapter 13

J ust before five bells, one of the ship's boys had raised a shout from the rigging where he had situated himself, and all hands had eagerly looked to the spot on the horizon where his hand pointed. In a moment, another shout went up, and the captain had his telescope trained on the sails of another ship of the fleet.

Signal flags flashed out, conveying the story of the night. No ships were lost, the fleet was reassembling, and they hoped to enter Mobile Bay by the next evening. As Gabriel had feared though, most of the fleet's supplies had been lost in the storm. None of the ships were designed for carrying an invading army, and all had been forced to stow supplies on deck, trusting to hope that they would avoid the very disaster that had befallen them.

The fleet gathered close in the afternoon, and the captains dined together with General Gálvez, conferring on strategy under the changed situation. After the conference ended and their captain had returned, Gabriel heard whispers among the crew that they had heard that Gálvez favored returning to New Orleans, to try their luck another time, but had been persuaded to land his invasion force against the hope that they could make do by plundering the British settlements outside of the reach of Fort Charlotte's protection.

In his heart, Gabriel was glad for this decision, for it would have been harder than the first time to have left Carlotta and the settlement for a second try at the invasion. And so the fleet continued to sail through the night for the great bay at Mobile.

Gabriel had never before been to Mobile—the British garrison there was not particularly friendly to Spanish ships, even merchant shipping—and he didn't know what to expect. He'd heard, though, that it was a very large, wonderfully sheltered expanse of water, and a fine place to drop anchor if one needed to ride out a storm on the Gulf of Mexico.

By the middle of the next day, it was painfully apparent that few of the captains of the fleet had experience with the entry to Mobile Bay, either. The great sheltering islands that made the bay so hospitable were formed of sand bars, deposited in the collision of the outflowing rivers of the bay and the waters of the Gulf. In addition to the islands that anyone could see, it soon developed that there were numerous bars just under the water, and none of the fleet's captains appeared to have navigated them before.

After several ships hit sandbars, and were able to get themselves back off with poles and patience, it came as no great surprise when word came that the *Volante* had run aground so far that no high tide would lift her clear, and as the tide fell, her keel broke, leading General Gálvez to order her abandoned. He was able to salvage her guns, though, swinging them over to his own flagship in slings, before the tide rose again and broke her up entirely.

He then ordered the fleet to back away from the bars until the next day, when they could, perhaps, get a better sense of where they were situated. The next morning, Gabriel was aboard one of a small flotilla of launches from the fleet, carefully taking soundings to guide the ships into the bay. Manuel was aboard another, and

Gabriel could see his friend directing the crew of his own launch with a calm, sure hand as they gathered the necessary information.

They rowed past the sad wreckage of the *Volante*, and Gabriel took heart in the knowledge that no men had been lost in the misadventure. Indeed, General Gálvez, returning to his usual energetic nature, sent a squad of his men ashore with the cannon from the lost ship, to set up a post guarding the entrance to the bay, so as to prevent any reinforcement of Fort Charlotte by sea from Pensacola.

The fleet anchored outside the bay, as Gálvez conferred with his captains and pondered how best to ensure that his invasion force could be safely landed to commence the attack on the fort. Nobody doubted that the British garrison was aware of their predicament and was making ready for their arrival, so any advantage of surprise was lost.

However, surprise was not necessarily a requirement to the success of their mission, and Gabriel heard scuttlebutt among the men that Gálvez had intelligence that suggested that the British garrison was undermanned and that reinforcements would have a very difficult time of it, should they attempt to travel by land.

On Gabriel's ship, the loss of their supplies was felt most keenly in the mess. The crew was on severely reduced rations, and even though an ongoing network of exchanges from one ship to another had evened out the supplies across the fleet, everyone was feeling the pinch of hunger. It was all the more galling to be standing at anchor just off what was obviously a bountiful land.

David from the village came to Gabriel and asked, "Why have those ashore not supplemented our supplies by hunting and trapping, now that they have the guns placed and earthworks raised about them?"

Gabriel shrugged. "They may well have done so, David, but do not forget that there are seven hundreds and more of us in the fleet, and even a determined effort to forage on the little point of land where they are emplaced will likely yield no more than they need to support their own numbers there."

David gave Gabriel a plaintive look and said, "But I am hungry, and what ship's biscuits we yet have are so hard as to nearly break my teeth."

"Be glad that the general prevailed upon the captains of the other ships, and they were willing to share what they had; we fared worse than most in the storm, and lost nearly all of our supplies."

David gave Gabriel a worried look and asked, "Will we have to turn back, then, for lack of food and powder?"

Gabriel clapped David on the back, smiling and shaking his head. "No, General Gálvez has dispatched an urgent request to Havana for reinforcements and replacement supplies, and there is every reason to hope that his prayers will be answered."

However, several days had passed since that dispatch with no reply from Havana and, privately, Gabriel believed that the dispatch might either have been intercepted by the British along the way, or else was hung up in the bureaucracy of Havana, the depths of which were legendary, even as far away as the river and New Orleans.

There was a shout from the lookout then, and Gabriel looked up to see signal flags flashing up from the general's ship. Within minutes, the message had been conveyed to the men—the fleet was to attempt the passage into the bay again, and they would wait no longer for reinforcements and resupply.

One at a time, each carefully following behind a launch which took constant soundings, the ships of the fleet picked their way through the complex sandbars to enter Mobile Bay. It was a slow passage, and Gálvez opted not to even convoy the ships behind a launch. Having lost one ship, he was reluctant to risk any more.

When night fell, though, all but three of the fleet lay safely within the protection of the great bay, and by six bells of the forenoon watch, the ships were all assembled in good order and ready to sail up the bay to begin the contest for Mobile.

Gabriel's ship was in the middle of the line, well behind the flagship, and nearly all eyes were on the general's ship. One of the sailors was watching aft, though, and cried out as a cutter swept into view around the point, flying the flag of Spain and flashing out signals as soon as it was recognized.

A buzz swept over the ship as the signals were read. Reinforcements from Havana were following, and would arrive the next day, carrying food and nearly doubling the size of their force.

David appeared before Gabriel, nearly crying with joy. "We shall have fresh meat, and rum, and—" he seized Gabriel and gave him a celebratory hug before dashing madly away to share the news further. Gabriel smiled, and felt more at ease than he had since the storm.

He greeted Hector Muñez, one of the hands on the ship, with a grin of his own. It was strange to him, being attached to the militia forces, rather than the ship's crew, but such were the results of the turns in his life of late. Hector had been one of the few members of the crew who had treated him as an equal in spite of his odd status aboard, and Gabriel appreciated the courtesy.

Hector smiled back at him, saying, "We shall surely prevail against the British now, do you not think?"

"Indeed, my friend, unless the garrison is many times larger than we expect, they will not be able to resist our attack. Of course, we do not know the ground here, and they have had all the time necessary to build up their defenses and preparations, so nothing is assured . . . but I cannot help but feel that God is smiling on our efforts here today."

Hector nodded enthusiastically. "I will be happy to be done with this affair, and to return to familiar ports. I know nobody in Mobile, nor in Pensacola, if we are truly to venture that far."

Gabriel smiled in reply, saying, "I have friends only in the river ports, and now, of course, among the settlements." He waved a hand toward the deck to encompass the men quartered there, and added, "I have also the duty of ensuring the safety of the friends I have accompanied on this voyage."

He sighed slightly, adding, "I know not how I am to see to their safety once this matter comes to a contest of arms, but I have made a commitment to a fierce woman back at their village, and I cannot fail her."

Hector gave him a knowing laugh. "Ah, a woman, eh? They can motivate us to do things that we thought were impossible, and reward us beyond mere riches when we succeed."

Gabriel frowned as he answered, "To be honest, Hector, I do not know what reward might await me with this woman. She is recently widowed, under circumstances that are both tragic and strange. It has affected her, and though she is certainly worthy of serving to my last breath, I do not think that she would welcome that sentiment at this time."

Hector shook his head slowly and sadly as he said, "Ah, my friend, you have found yourself in a difficult position indeed. It is so much simpler to manage your affairs as I do, with but ladies who are friends in the various ports that I frequent, and no entanglements or commitments." He laughed at his own comments until he saw the expression on Gabriel's face.

"Oh, I meant no offense, my friend. It's only that—"

"I take no offense, Hector. I only recognize my own policy, up until the time when I met this woman. She is like a fever that I cannot shake, both unwelcome and unwelcoming, and yet, strangely irresistible. I will confess that my thoughts return to her more often than I would like, and I have completely forgotten the lady friends that I once had in the trade, in favor of wondering what will happen upon my return to her."

He made a sour face. "All of this assumes, of course, that our General Gálvez can repeat his performance at Fort Bute in the coming days, and that he can bring us through this contest without sustaining serious harm."

Hector placed his hand on Gabriel's arm and gave him a confident nod. "I am sure, my friend, that if anyone can do it, the general is the man. I have followed his career since his days as an instructor at the academy of Ávila—my cousin studied under him, and had only praise for the man. When I learned that he had been posted as governor to Louisiana, I rejoiced in my heart for the knowledge that his administration would be wise and practical."

He shrugged. "So far, I have not been disappointed. He has promoted trade about the Spanish holdings in the Gulf, which has meant plenty of work for the likes of you and me. His cordons against the British smuggling operations have been a source of increased profit as well, and you are even more familiar than I with his success as a military commander."

Gabriel nodded in agreement, saying, "I know that fortune has favored him before now, and it seems that it is lining up with him again in this, yet I know also that fortune may be fickle, and that it is wise not to count any feat as completed until the sun has set over the field of victory."

"You are wise in this, my friend, yet I think that you have every reason to expect that you will return to this woman who bedevils you . . . so you had best be prepared for the consequences of our victory." Hector flashed him another grin. "Sometimes, it is more difficult to succeed than to fail."

Gabriel smiled wryly and replied, "Indeed, but I will accept that difficulty. Thank you, my friend, and may the Blessed Virgin watch over you in the days to come."

Hector replied, "And you, my friend," and both men turned to go back to their respective duties as the ship made fast for another night at anchor.

Chapter 14

In the morning, the crew and the villagers shared a last meager meal of hardtack, soaked in a bit of grog to make it both easier on the teeth and somewhat more palatable. The meal was more bearable in the sure knowledge that fresh supplies were en route and would, indeed, arrive with the tide.

David could still be heard over the general conversation of the mess, complaining about the food, but even his complaints had a less serious edge to them, and seemed to be mainly for form. When, just after two bells of the afternoon watch, the first sails of the ships from Havana were spotted coming around the point to await guidance through the treacherous bar, David was the first to volunteer as an oarsman, hoping for a meal aboard one of the ships of salvation by way of reward.

His hopes were not immediately realized, though, as another ship of the Havana squadron stood to outside the bar as soon as the first had sailed to anchor beside Gálvez' flagship. The hapless villager wound up pulling at the oars for most of the afternoon, until he was relieved by the next launch and returned to his ship to enjoy a meal along with his messmates, including fresh fruit in abundance, a healthy ration of ale, and even a bit of meat in his potato stew.

After he had wolfed down his dinner, he leaned back and belched, and then grinned at Gabriel, who was favoring him with a mild look of disgust. "Ay, my friend, if you work so hard for all of a day, and return to experience a meal such as this at the end of your day, then I shall excuse you fully, should your belly be heard from in an inappropriate manner."

Gabriel shook his head, smiling slightly, and returned to his conversation with the ship's master, one Roger Cooper, who had jumped ship from a British merchantman and had fetched up in Havana. After a period of a year or two, during which he'd learned Spanish, the man had volunteered to serve in the Spanish Navy, and had quickly risen through the ranks to become the master of this small sloop.

Because of his irregular past, he had told Gabriel that he would never command a Spanish ship of his own, nor even serve at the helm of anything with more than two masts, but he was content with his place, and he and Gabriel had struck up a rapport that might even be called a friendship. Gabriel appreciated Roger's frank assessment of situations as they presented themselves, and Roger was inclined by nature to regard Gabriel as the de facto leader of the villagers' militia.

They were discussing how best to land the men and materiel of the invasion force from his ship. "This ship's draft is not extreme," said the master, "and yet, I should like to avoid any contact with the ocean floor. We shall have to use the launches, unless we should happen to secure a port with proper docking facilities . . . without we have landed our forces yet."

Gabriel sighed, "We shall have to land in order to secure the port, in all probability, and yet until we have secured a port, the landing will be far more difficult than it would otherwise be."

"Particularly with our holds full of landlubbers," Roger

answered, and then quickly touched his knuckle to his forehead in the English manner, adding, "Meaning no disrespect, but transferring those who have not the sea legs nor any particular skill at swarming down the shrouds into a launch will inevitably mean that some of them, at least, will wind up in the water."

He looked thoughtful and said, "Not but what some of them wouldn't be improved by a dunking." Gabriel frowned at him for a moment, and then started laughing.

"I cannot deny that the odor has been quite close below decks," he answered, adding, "We should like some more fresh water, that we might clean ourselves by less extreme measures than by being dropped between the ship and the boat."

"Fresh water will still be rationed until we have secured a beachhead," the master averred, adding, "salt water will serve nearly as well, in any event."

Gabriel shook his head, saying, "Not in my experience. Why, even river mud will dry and flake off of a man's skin. Salt leaves one feeling crisp and starched, which is fine for a uniform, but not so appealing on one's hair and face."

Roger smiled in response and said, "We shall have the water we need, not only for drinking, but for the luxury of bathing, in short order. We have but to finish reconnoitering the bay and environs, and then the general will select a location, and we shall land on it, taking it by force if necessary."

Gabriel shot him a look of friendly frustration, and the master smiled again, concluding, "It will be but a few days more now, and then you will all sleep on solid ground."

Gabriel nodded conceding the point, and walked away, frowning to himself. How had things come to such a pass that he was pleased with the prospect of sleeping anywhere but on his ship? In part, he supposed, he was eager to prove himself among these men who had served already under enemy fire, while he had laid in a bed, waiting for his bones to knit.

He wondered, too, if a part of it was related to the mystery that was his relationship—if it could even bear up under the weight of that name!—with Carlotta. He'd seen other sailors suddenly lose their desire to stay on the water, favoring instead the stability of hearth and home.

They would pine while afloat, and only seemed truly to be happy when they were homeward bound. Many gave up their shipboard lives in favor of careers on land, but when Gabriel had visited them, there was always a wistfulness about them for the wind and the sail, no matter how content they were in their new lives.

Of course, many sailors had a house ashore and wives and children, too, yet remained as itinerant residents in their own homes. The rest of the time, they were men of the sea, with no more commitment to their vows than the basest bachelor in their company. Gabriel had little respect nor patience for such men, and knew in his heart that he would do better, though he did not look forward to the alternatives of being ever homesick, whether for the sea or for home.

Gabriel shook himself, blinking hard. Carlotta had given him no cause to be thinking in these terms, and he had much yet to do before he could return to her and learn whether she ever would.

General Gálvez kept the fleet at anchor for several more days, as Roger had predicted. There was no doubt that the British defenders at Fort Charlotte, sited far enough up river that an overland approach would be necessary, were aware of their presence in the bay—more than once, the launches scouting about the shoreline of the great body of water had reported seeing movement ashore.

Some was doubtless merely wildlife, but on several occasions, men had been clearly seen. Whether the men were Indians or British scouts, or even settlers, Gálvez' plans were not laid with any dependence whatever on an element of surprise.

Finally, Gálvez selected a landing site at the mouth of the next river to the western side of the bay from where Fort Charlotte lay. By avoiding any lengthy and chancy river crossings, he hoped to preserve his force's energy for the assault on the fort itself.

As Roger had envisioned, there was no means of landing the men from most of the ships directly ashore, and so a flotilla of launches shuttled back and forth from morning until the sun's rays slanted steeply across the water of the bay, ferrying the men to land, and then the cannon that they would haul behind them, and the gear and supplies that they would need to house and victual the men.

Gabriel was almost immediately engaged in directing his friends as they raised rough tents, and missed the excitement caused when a ragged-looking man emerged from the mangroves and approached the landing force.

Someone shouted out, and as heads turned, more than one man reached for a weapon to confront the stranger. He stopped and raised his hands and called out in English. Gabriel and his companions could not make out what he was trying to say, but the ship's master happened to be ashore, and he came bustling up from where he had been helping unload a launch.

"He says that he was a member of the British militia at the

fort, but that he has come to offer us information and assistance."
He called back to the deserter in his own tongue, and the deserter
answered in kind. He nodded and beckoned the man forward.

"Somebody fetch him something to eat, and send word for
General Gálvez. Tell him that this man offers himself on parole as
a prisoner, and is able to tell us of the forces and their disposition
within Fort Charlotte." The ragged militia man stepped forward,
keeping his hands before him and smiling reassuringly.

Though their weapons were put away, many of the members
of the invasion force kept hands on hilts and stocks, wary that a
man who offered to betray one side might well betray the other in
turn. The man looked nervously back at the many pairs of eyes
that regarded him with suspicion, and seemed grateful when Roger
placed an arm on his shoulder in a protective gesture.

"Come," he said in Spanish, as much for the benefit of the
invaders as for his captive, "Let us go and meet with the general."

Later, sitting with Gabriel at supper, the ship's master
seemed scarcely able to contain himself, so excited was he at what
he had learned. Finally, he couldn't restrain himself any longer and,
looking from side to side to be sure that nobody else could hear, he
leaned forward and said quietly, "You cannot breathe a word of
this until the general has posted our orders, but having that deserter
come forward to us was a stroke of divine providence."

Gabriel leaned in and motioned with his hand for the ship's
master to continue. The man grinned and said, "Every detail that
he gave us about the British forces matched what our scouts have
reported, and what's more, he was able to provide us marvelous
intelligence about the state of the troops within the fort, beyond
their mere disposition."

He waved his hand over the encampment and said, "A mere three hundred men guard the fortification—a quarter of what we have here assembled—and while its commander has sent to Pensacola for reinforcements as soon as our fleet was spotted at the mouth of the bay, the way overland from there is difficult, and there was little hope among the men within the fort that they will be reinforced, either from Pensacola or from their allies among the Indians in these parts."

Gabriel nodded closing his eyes and breathing deeply of the evening breeze blowing out to sea, and carrying the scent of the wooded bottomlands. Looking up at Roger, he said, "Almost, I can begin to believe, my friend, that we have nothing to fear in this engagement. With this intelligence, we should readily prevail, and, having done so, strike a blow that will make our next assault on the British outposts here all the more likely to find success."

He inhaled deeply again and asked, "What drove the Englishman to desert? Was he merely shy of the coming conflict, or did he quarrel with his commander, or was there some other cause?"

The ship's master shook his head. "It is always difficult to say what drives a man to treachery. He was not a part of the force dispatch here from Britain, but a militia man recruited—or impressed—from the local population."

His face worked briefly as he thought about the question, and then he said, "Perhaps we will have an opportunity to ask him when this is all over. For now, I am content that he is our man, and that the information he has given us will prove to be the last piece in the general's strategy."

He nodded and added, "It is getting late, and this has been

a day of great labor and great events. We would both do well to retire early, to prepare ourselves for what the morrow will bring."

Gabriel smiled across the table at his friend and stood, saying, "You are wiser than you even give yourself credit for. Sleep well, and let us hope for a swift conclusion to this matter."

Chapter 15

The next morning dawned clear, with mist rising into the still air from the mangrove swamps that lay thickly about the encampment. As the watch woke the rest of the men in the camp, Gabriel stretched languorously before rising from his jumbled blanket on the ground. Nearby, David was sitting up from his bedroll and blinking at the morning light.

"What say you, David," Gabriel called out to him, "Shall we go forth today and take some more territory from the British for the sake of our Governor and King?"

David favored Gabriel with a sardonic glance, and Gabriel laughed in reply. "Come, my friend, let us see what there might be available to break our fast this morning."

David perked up somewhat at that, and stood up, saying, "That is how I should prefer to be greeted in the morning, by all means." He yawned widely and scratched his nose, complaining, "I was having a wonderful dream, too, of Consuela's *ropa viejo* ... I could nearly taste the peppers and feel the stock running down my chin ..."

He sighed, and Gabriel made a face. "Yes, David, watching you eat is enough to cure most hungers, but I have not dined since last night, so let us see what there is to eat, even though it will not be so fine as Consuela's cooking."

The two made their way to the canteen, where steam rose in

great clouds from cauldrons of the tiresome beans and rice, the same staples as were the daily ration while the expedition was underway. Previous encounters with the cook, though, had taught even David to refrain from so much as rolling his eyes, never mind making comments, so long as the irascible man could see or hear.

Once they'd carried their rations away to sit together and eat, though, David gave voice to his frustrations, his voice quiet to start, but growing louder as he warmed to his subject. "Have we left all of the fresh victuals on board the ships? Could not the cook have added so much as a sour slice of bacon to the beans? Has nobody found any meat or greens in this place yet? Why, I can hear all manner of beasts in the wood behind us, yet here we have the same old flavorless beans and bug-infested rice."

Gabriel grinned at his friend. "You complain that the beans have not enough meat, and the rice has too much? Make up your mind, my friend!"

David spluttered in reply, "With the resupply from Havana, should they not have also brought ashore some fresh meat, and perhaps some rice that has not yet been enhanced by the addition of vermin?"

Gabriel shrugged broadly. "They may well have, but he may be saving the newer goods for those from whom he does not hear complaints." He nodded over toward where the cook stood glaring at them through the steam of his cauldrons, a ladle held with what could only be interpreted as menace in his white-knuckled hand.

David glanced over and raised his hands placatingly to the cook, sighing and turning back to Gabriel. "I cannot help it; I am accustomed to eating somewhat better than this, even in the lean times that I have sometimes known."

Gabriel nodded in agreement. "I understand, but you can be glad that we eat as well as we do. There have been times and places where men such as ourselves have faced far worse privations than we do here."

David sighed and grumbled, "I am going to see if I may go out after we eat to try to catch something decent for our camp, at least. The swamps behind here are loud with birds and there are bound to be alligators, even one of which would feed many people."

Gabriel smiled and said, "I do not anticipate that you will encounter any resistance to that plan, though I suspect that the alligator would be better-equipped to hunt you in his own environment than the other way around. You should also be cautious about firing a shot without all about being aware of your plans."

David grunted in response, clearly less interested in the practicalities of the hunt than in the prospect of real food on the table. He turned back to his breakfast, mechanically chewing and swallowing.

As the men cleared their bowls, Roger walked up with his own and asked, "May I join you fine gentlemen on this lovely morning with this wonderful repast?"

David rolled his eyes at Gabriel, who grinned back and replied, "You certainly may, my friend. What has you in such fine spirits today?"

The ship's master settled himself down and smiled beatifically. "You know as well as I that I cannot delve too deeply into the details, Gabriel, but I am filled with anticipation for the events of the days to come."

David gave both men a puzzled look and stood, saying, "I have never understood people who could crack a smile upon first rising. I am going to go and make my apologies to the cook, and see whether I can sweet-talk him into granting me a second serving."

Gabriel laughed, saying, "The food is so terrible that you cannot help but beg for another helping? That's an odd way to approach the argument, but I do look forward to hearing how your request is received."

They watched the young man go and speak with the cook, who glowered at him at first, and then broke out in a great grin, and ladled more beans into David's bowl. David returned, looking somewhat less grim than before.

"I told him that as I had eaten more of the first serving, it had tasted increasingly better with each bite, and that by the time I finished a second, I should have no choice but to praise his work to all who could hear me speak."

Gabriel and Roger laughed and David gave them an ever so slightly smug look before continuing into his meal.

Roger turned then to Gabriel, saying, "I should like for you to meet this British deserter. Though he does not speak our language yet, he was most engaging as he conversed with the governor, and by the end of the discussion was even venturing to say a few words for himself."

He chuckled, continuing, "His accent, of course, is a terrible thing to hear, but he seems to be a quick-minded and pleasant fellow. I think you would like him quite well, and I would be glad to serve as his translator, if you're interested."

Gabriel nodded, saying, "I am always happy to meet someone

who has left hardship for hardship, and who yet maintains a cheerful and pleasant demeanor. I must imagine that it is a difficult thing to turn on your King when all your neighbors support the crown and many of them even go so far as to volunteer in his service."

He frowned and asked, "Is there no objection from the general to this man speaking to those outside of the men entrusted with our strategy, however?"

Roger answered, "When I spoke with the general a few minutes ago, asking whether we might need to reprise our interview with this deserter, he gave me to believe that he thought that the man seemed intimidated by his high position in this army, and that speaking with men of his own rank might reveal more than further discussions with the commanders."

Smiling, he continued, "Indeed, I confess, I am making use of you in this regard, as there are few who can be both spared and trusted."

Gabriel laughed, motioning at his leg, and said, "Ah, then, my infirmity is the reason for my selection in this duty, then. Very well, bring him on, and let us see what we may learn from him that the general has so far failed to."

"I shall go and get him, then," Roger said, "just as soon as I have finished with this meal." He turned to David, adding with a twinkle in his eye, "You are right, my friend, it does grow better tasting with each bite!"

David again rolled his eyes, grumbling under his breath to himself about the decency of people who were so cheerful before the sun had even fully risen. Before he could finish his second serving, a sergeant came around and impressed him into a squad to work on the effort of getting the cannon ashore, and David grouchily stood to join the man, leaving Roger and Gabriel with an admonition, "Don't let anyone eat my beans."

Gabriel waved in assurance, torn between wishing that he could help in the effort and being glad that the state of his still-healing leg excused him from such heavy duty. He knew that his services had been useful shipboard, and felt certain that he would again be of use once any siege began, but in the part of the expedition that called for heavy work—men's work—he felt as though his fellows were carrying him along to humor him.

Though Roger made light of it, and indeed now attempted to cast it as an advantage, the thought gave Gabriel no cheer, and he frowned to himself, responding automatically to Roger's comments regarding the handling of the ships, each in their turn, as they stood to anchor for unloading.

"There, that one ought to bring our friend David some relief," he said, waving his hand at a ship—one of the new additions from Havana to the fleet—as it dropped anchor and its ship's launches were lowered into the water.

Gabriel quirked an eyebrow at Roger. "How is that, then?"

"I have spoken to the master on that ship, and he mentioned to me that they have a great supply of livestock on board, mainly hogs. He was complaining about the smell below decks, and was pleased at the thought that they'd be unloaded soon, and turned into food for the army."

Gabriel smiled and remarked, "And so there will shortly be an answer to both men's complaints. It is good to see two problems solve each other so neatly. Would that that were the case more broadly, as in the contest of arms that we soon face."

The ship's master gave him a sly smile, and said mysteriously, "We shall see, my friend. I have a feeling that our English deserter may prove to be the key to making that happen. Let me go and bring him here now, and you shall see for yourself."

Roger stood and shortly returned with the English deserter. The man looked far better today than he had the previous day, having had a chance to shave and wash. With a flourish of his hand, the ship's master said to Gabriel, "My friend, allow me to present Thomas Grant, a tanner, late of Mobile town, now in the service of our cause and King."

Gabriel stood and bowed deeply to the man, saying, "It is an honor to meet you, Thomas. May your service in this matter be successful and your rewards great." He waited for Roger to translate, and then added, "We were gratified to learn that the challenges that face us here appear to place this garrison within our power to overcome."

After listening to Roger's translation, Thomas nodded, looking about him at the dense crowd of shelters and tents housing the invasion force on the beach. He answered, and Roger translated, "It is likewise a pleasure to meet you, and I do hope that the intelligence that I bring with me is useful in your attempt to overcome the fort here, with, I pray, a minimum loss of life."

Gabriel nodded in reply, closing his eyes briefly and crossing himself. "I share your hope that we are not forced to reduce the contest to a matter of piling up corpses on both sides." He regarded the man closely, adding, "There has been enough death and loss in all of our lives of late."

Shaking his head to dispel the gloomy mood that threatened to descend with these reflections, he motioned for both men to sit, and once all three of them were comfortable, he said, "I cannot help but be curious as to what would drive you to quit your countrymen in favor of an invading force. Why did you choose to join our side of the fight?"

As he listened to Roger translate the question, Thomas smiled, shaking his head slightly, and then answered through Roger, "Everyone I speak with has the same question for me, and I will tell you what I have told everyone else as well. It is a long story, which I have only had time to outline in the briefest of all possible tellings, but I know that Roger is particularly interested—" Roger interjected as he translated, "Yes, I certainly am," before continuing with Thomas' comments, "and so I would be glad to tell you of it, if you have the time."

Gabriel glanced around the encampment and replied, "As I remain on light duty, due to a fracture of the leg that I sustained in a storm late last year, I am of no use as the men move heavy equipment and weaponry that we have brought with us. Tell your tale, and let us learn from it."

Thomas smiled in response and launched into his story. "My family came here from the Georgia colony nearly four years ago, after the various Committees of Safety and Continental Congresses had whipped the population into a ridiculous passion, and spurred them to take the absurd action of declaring independence against the English crown."

He grimaced, continuing, "As my father has always been a staunch and vocal supporter of the King, our property was threatened with confiscation, and we feared for our safety. When a group of hoodlums broke into the powder magazine in Savannah and stole the powder for their own uses, we began to think that we might have to leave our home entirely."

"My father resisted for as long as he could, until we received word of the obnoxious and ill-mannered attempt by the Continental Congress to tell all the world of how abused they had felt at the hands of the King."

He snorted, adding, "They brought half of it upon themselves, by being obstinate about paying the costs of our defense to a Parliament that had sprung to their aid on any number of occasions. The ingratitude that dripped from every word of their self-styled 'declaration of independency' was nauseating to people like my father."

Throwing up his hands, he sighed, "Alas, all too many of our neighbors in Georgia did not see things this way, and they formed militias and committees and sent representatives to the Provincial Congress, and supported the formation of a rebel government, raised a militia and continued to arm themselves ever more menacingly."

"My father argued long into the night on more than one evening with his friends, convincing some, but losing others to the clutches of the rebels and their denial of responsibility to the duties demanded of them by their sovereign."

Gabriel nodded in sympathy to this point and said, "Those same duties are what bring many of us here. I do believe that we would all rather be tending to our own affairs than fighting against other men who would likewise prefer to be just left alone. And yet, when our sovereign calls us to action, we have no choice but to answer."

Thomas nodded agreement, continuing, "That the rebels shied away from performing duties so light as merely paying the financial costs of providing for their own safety was particularly repugnant to people like my father, when we considered what the King and Parliament had every right to demand of us."

Shaking his head angrily, he said, "No matter how persuasively my father spoke, however, the malcontents in our colony continued on their heedless path to a confrontation with the King. Once they had the upper hand, they let loose the worst elements among them to harry and abuse we who remained loyal."

He shrugged, his face still clouded at remembered anger and pain. "So we all came here to seek the safety and society of those who yet swore loyalty to the Crown. My brother and his wife saw their house fired before we left, and escaped with just the clothes on their back and their twin babies in their arms."

Grimacing, he continued. "My father has said to him that we stayed too long, but he believes that we stayed just long enough to see the true natures of these rebels, who claim to fight for freedom while employing the most brutal of force to achieve their ends."

He paused for a long moment, rubbing his forehead in grief. "My wife fell ill on the journey, and died of a fever not long after we arrived here. She gave me no children before her death, and I blame the rebels for denying me the joy of bringing them into the world with her."

Looking back up and taking a deep breath to steady himself, he went on with his story. "The people of this colony have been most welcoming, but the privations of the war have worn heavily on us all."

Motioning to the bay, he said, "Shipping has been disrupted, between the privateers that prowl the Gulf of Mexico, and the redirection of supplies to support the troops of the British forces, and so it has been difficult for any to eke out a living here. For those of us who are newly arrived, it is an even greater challenge, for who would chose to give their business to someone strange to them over a friend whom they have known for decades?"

Patting his lean belly, the deserter said, "There have been plenty of times that the only food that was to be had was what we grew ourselves, and there, too, the people who know this territory best are at an advantage."

He frowned now and tossed his head in the direction of the town, to the north. "As soon as he received word that the Spaniards had joined with the French in backing the rebels, the commander of the local garrison asked all of us of fighting age to join into his service in the fort, promising both rewards for our loyalty, and regular meals. I answered his call, of course, as did my brother and my father."

"It is for them that I have come to your aid."

Gabriel frowned in confusion, and even Roger stumbled over the translation, giving Thomas a quizzical look and asking him in his own language for clarification, saying to Gabriel, "No, he says that he can explain what he means," and then listening to the rest of Thomas' next comment before continuing to translate.

"It is no secret that you have come here with a mighty force, in comparison to our garrison of British regulars and militias. Many of us in the fort heard word of ship after ship after ship of the Spanish fleet entering the bay, and when my friend, who is a scout in the militia, came back and told us of how many men these ships carried . . . " he shrugged. "I could only think that we would all be killed, if we did not surrender. The commander of the garrison, Captain Durnford, has a great estate not far from here, and has insisted that we can hold this place, no matter how large your Spanish forces are."

Shrugging again, he said, "By giving you as much intelligence as I can about the fort and who its defenders are, I hope to cause him to surrender peacefully, that my brother and father may survive and we may all live in such peace as the Spanish governor will permit. They say that he is a very civilized and cultured man, and this gives me hope that we may live unmolested once he has prevailed here."

Roger nodded, and Gabriel looked thoughtful, before asking, "Do you think that your Captain Durnford is likely to surrender without contesting his position under arms?"

Thomas looked at him, motioning helplessly with his hands, and replied through Roger, "I do not know, but I do know that if I did not make this attempt, and my brother's children grew up without knowing their father or grandfather, I would never be at rest myself. It was the best plan I could arrive at under the circumstances, and I did not consult with them before I fled."

He looked down at his hands bleakly. "I only hope that they understand that I have made this sacrifice in an attempt to ensure their safety, and do not think too ill of me for betraying the Crown on their behalf."

Looking back up at them, his voice took on a tone of pleading as he said, "Do you think that your Governor Gálvez can make Captain Durnford see the reason in laying down arms?"

Roger answered before Gabriel could make any response, and then turned back to Gabriel, translating his own words, "I told him that although I know not, if anyone can perform such a feat, it is our governor."

Gabriel nodded somberly, and placed a hand on the English

deserter's shoulder and looking into the man's eyes. "Tell him that I think that his brother and father would appreciate the personal sacrifices that he has made, if they could but hear him describe what he has done for them, and see in his eyes the knowledge of what he has given up for their safety."

Turning back to Roger, he said, "I am not convinced that he will be entirely our man, however, and I do believe that he should be maintained under guard in our camp. If he sees an opportunity to ensure the safe escape of his family by betraying us, I have no doubt that he will leap at that chance. We need to be certain that he never gets that opportunity."

Roger nodded sadly, and translated only Gabriel's comforting words for Thomas, keeping his private thoughts as to the deserter's reliability to himself. Thomas smiled in response to Gabriel's comment to him, and Gabriel could see unshed tears in the man's eyes.

Roger rose, offering Thomas his hand to help him up from his seat as well. "I should see our guest back to his quarters," he said to Gabriel, who smiled at both men before turning back to regard his empty bowl, already deep in thought about Thomas' history and what it might mean for the expedition.

Chapter 16

All through the day, the men continued to bring ashore the big guns and stores to supply them. The encampment grew ever larger as well, as the last of the troops disembarked their ships. When the final cannon had been unloaded late in the day, the order came to make ready for the march to the fort, some ten miles away.

The next morning, the forces broke camp, leaving behind a makeshift field hospital, and such forces as the general thought necessary to protect their potential retreat, should something unexpected happen at the fort.

A galley had rowed north in the evening dusk, carrying the first load of men to the position that Gálvez had chosen for their assault on the fort, but had returned in the night, badly mauled by cannon fire from the fort. One man had died from wounds sustained in the attack, a splinter from the smashed side of the ship driven right through him, but they had suffered no other significant losses.

However, it was clear that there was nothing for it but to approach the enemy fort overland, despite the slow pace that would impose, and the tiresome labor it would entail.

Just behind the scouts who ranged through the woods, looking for both enemy troops and the best path through the mire of the bottomland, a group of well-rested, heavily-built young men wielded axes to clear the road to the town. They left a pathway just wide enough for the cannon crews to haul their heavy charges on carts, weaving their way between the stumps, and doing their best to simply keep moving, as any pause gave the wheels time to sink into the soft ground.

David limped beside Gabriel, silent, for once, about the quality of their latest meal. It had been scarcely any better—the cook had orders to make the livestock last as long as he could, and the man's nature was to be overcautious in these matters, anyway. As a result, only one hog had been butchered before camp was broken, and its meat had been nearly undetectable in their beans.

A cannon ball had rolled from its cart while he was unloading one of the launches the previous day and had landed directly beside his foot, after rebounding against the man's leg. While he wasn't badly hurt, it was enough to put him beside Gabriel instead of on the shaft of a cart, hauling a cannon. Lost in thought, a dour look on his face, he was not the most cheerful companion, but Gabriel was thankful at least that he wasn't complaining aloud.

They also were not entirely unladen as they trudged along together. Each carried, in addition to his personal knapsack, a share of the powder for the cannon, in a bag slung over their shoulders. It both mollified their pride and also removed some of the burden from the wheels of the cannon-carts, helping to keep them from sinking too far into soft spots on the road.

Their progress was slow, however, between needing to wait for the road to be cleared, and then waiting for the cannon crews to make their way through the rough path, and finally, the many men on foot behind the cannon. By the time the day was out, they had, Gabriel noted, gone just outside the sound of the waves on the beach.

He had wondered idly why they were not simply marching on the beach, and then he saw a crew falter under the shafts of one of the cannon carts as it pulled with a great wet sound from the muck over which they were dragging it. As bad as this passage might be, the carts would never have moved over the sand at all—indeed, he remembered watching crews carry them on their shoulders from the launches, prior to loading the cannon onto them.

Not for the last time, he was grateful that his labor could be spared in these incredible tasks, while at the same time feeling a sense of shame that he walked nearly unburdened as his fellow soldiers struggled against such challenges.

David, limping beside him as the leaders of the column gave the word to stop for this day, gave voice to his thoughts, saying, "I am not so much unhappy that others labor in my place as I am glad that there are sufficient numbers here that my labor is not too sorely missed."

Gabriel smiled at his friend and replied, "Well said, my friend. Hopefully, this will turn out to be well-worth the hard work and sacrifice of our fellows." He looked around at the sweating and weary men about him and added, "I am certain that it will, as dedicated as we all are to this effort."

The next day was more of the same, and the day after, and the day after that. On the final afternoon of their journey, Thomas and Roger strode up from the rear of the column, and Roger stopped by where Gabriel was helping a crew re-pack the axle of a cart with fresh lard.

"Thomas tells me that we are approaching the fort and the town now, and we are going to the general to provide intelligence as to where he believes we might best situate ourselves to effect the surrender of the forces within."

Gabriel straightened up and wiped his brow. "That is welcome news indeed, my friend. Have you learned anything further about the circumstances of our guide's arrival in our ranks? We must remain alert to the possibility that he was sent to misdirect us, and cause us to place our forces such that they might be overwhelmed or vulnerable to ambush."

Roger shook his head, smiling. "No, I believe that he is sincere in wanting to see us prevail as quickly as possible here, and he knows well that Havana would send more forces to avenge us, should there be any trickery in his advice. In addition, the general has vetted his intelligence against what we have been able to learn independent of his word, and is well-satisfied that he has provided us trustworthy information."

He shrugged and added, "And if not, we will know soon enough, and we will find a different way to overcome the enemy in this contest. We have the advantage of men, we have a seasoned and brilliant leader, we're well supplied, and we have every indication that God Himself has smiled upon our prospects here."

Gabriel sighed gustily. "I hope that you are right in this, my friend. It is worse, this waiting for the blow to strike, than it is to recover afterward." He rubbed his face thoughtfully, gazing at the silent English deserter and said, "We must each keep watch for any sign of trickery, as we act on the guidance that Thomas has offered us."

Then, addressing Thomas through Roger, he said, "We owe you a debt of gratitude for the intelligence you have offered us, and we each look forward no less eagerly than you to the conclusion of this affair. I wish you the joy of a swift reunion with your brother and father, and pray that they will see the wisdom of your actions."

Bowing his head to both men, he added, "Now, I must beg your indulgence as I attend to my duty here." Roger tilted his head in answer, smiling, and led Thomas again toward the head of the column as Gabriel turned back to slathering the thick lard into the axle, pondering anew all that Thomas had told them, trying to think of what key piece of information he might have revealed that could be of use to their forces.

The army spent the next few days building up their encampment, just beyond sight of the fort. The artillery pieces were drawn closer in, and the general directed crews to begin construction of six emplacements, sited to give them a clear shot at the walls of the fort. Late in the evening, Roger sought out Gabriel, carrying a sheet of paper and fairly bursting with laughter.

"You must hear this, Gabriel. It is the letter that General Gálvez has had sent under a flag to this Captain Durnford in the fort." He held up the page before him and read.

"Sir: If I had fewer than two thousand men under my command—" Gabriel interjected, "but we number no more than twelve hundreds," and Roger motioned him into silence with his hand, continuing to read, "—and if you had more than one hundred soldiers and a few sailors, I would not ask you to surrender, but the great inequality of forces compels us—you to yield immediately—" Gabriel snorted, and Roger frowned at him, silencing him again. "—or I to make you bear all the extremities of war if a useless and uncalled-for resistance irritates the patience of my troops, too much annoyed by some accidents. To-day I am ready to grant you a regular capitulation and in accordance with circumstances; tomorrow perhaps nothing will be left to you but the sterile repentance of not having accepted my proposition in favor of the unfortunates who are under your command. I have the honor to be, et cetera, et cetera."

Gabriel could hardly contain himself, exclaiming, "Our general is a bold and even hilarious fellow. He inflates our numbers and discounts the enemy's by two thirds, which is a pretty trick for certain. What accidents have we suffered, that he mentions?"

Roger waved his hand dismissively, saying, "I have not heard of any, but then I am hardly privy to the counsels of the general's senior staff."

Gabriel gave him a frown and replied, "Indeed, I find that I wonder how you have happened upon a copy of the very letter sent to the enemy commander? Are you not now attached somehow to the general's staff?"

Roger shrugged modestly. "Ah, well, there was some consideration given to transmitting the letter to the captain of the fort in English, but in the end, the general decided that it would be more in keeping with the practices of diplomacy to send it in French instead. He gave me leave to share the original with those whom I saw fit, as it can only give heart to our forces."

He waved the letter in the air and added, "I thought that you might appreciate hearing how our general addresses the enemy commander. It is my hope that the captain in his fort will see the wisdom of his proposition, and will command his troops to lay down their arms and accept that they have been beaten by a superior force."

Gabriel nodded thoughtfully. "We may hope for such an

outcome, yes, but we must also be ready for the possibility that the British at Pensacola will find some way to provide reinforcement here, and make this into a real contest. Should they even the numbers to any meaningful degree, this could become a field of blood."

Roger replied, "The difficulty of performing such a feat is severe, and the general has acted with such energetic efficiency as to make the course of surrender an honorable one for our enemy." He shrugged. "We should have our answer by the morning; the general has sent Colonel Bouligny over with it, and I believe that the colonel is well-acquainted with Captain Durnford."

Gabriel laughed, "I do not expect that the general will make so free with that reply, unless it should be a complete capitulation."

Roger smiled in reply, and said, "He is remarkably open with his staff as to the state of our advantage. I will grant you that I have yet to see how he treats them when there is adverse information to be shared, but it is my sense of the man that he tends to be well-enough pleased with our chances that we will learn of the enemy's reply as soon as he has it, regardless of its content."

Gabriel dipped his head, acquiescing to the other man's better knowledge of the general's character. "No matter what their reply, we shall have some new work to do on the morrow, so we had best get what rest we can tonight."

Roger chuckled, saying, "You sound like an old mariner, my friend, always focused on getting your rest when you can."

"How else could I be?" Gabriel grinned. "In any event, you cannot argue the point with me—tomorrow will not be a day of rest, but a day of preparation for battle or acceptance of prisoners, occupation of their fort, assessment of their positions and so on.

Either way, plenty of work."

Roger stood and bowed slightly, saying, "I will leave you to it, then, my friend. May you sleep deeply and wake ready for whatever the morrow may bring."

Gabriel waved a farewell to his friend, and settled down in his bedroll, willing himself to sleep. The stars overhead twinkled merrily, almost seeming to join in the laughter that Roger had in his voice at the missive the general had sent to his adversary and, after a bit, Gabriel could almost hear their tinkling giggles at the ridiculous little struggles that they were witness to among mortal men.

Late in the night, he became aware that he had been joined by the presence of someone else. It was Carlotta, who smiled at him as he gazed at her. Even though she was trying to give the appearance of calm happiness, he could tell by her manner that she was worried and sad. She was silent, and offered no reproach, but looked to his belt to confirm that her father's dagger still resided there.

Satisfied with Gabriel's safety, she turned to leave, but came back as he called out to her. "How fares the village?"

She did not answer in words, but nodded slowly, giving him reassurance that all was well in the absence of the men of the militia, as well as his absence. He frowned at her refusal to speak aloud—she had never lacked for words before, to his recollection—but asked, "Have you found the necessary assistance to get on with the new season's work?"

She nodded again, and then smiled tolerantly, and shook her head at his irrelevant questions. She turned and walked away, giving him a teasing smile over her shoulder. She had just dropped the shift from her shoulders when Gabriel sat upright, covered in sweat, and realized that he had been lost in a dream, the product of his own thoughts and desires, and he reminded himself that he had no certain knowledge that she shared any of those, aside from her interest in seeing him and the rest of the men of the village returned home safely.

Still, as he rolled over to go back to sleep, he found himself wishing that she had been facing him when she disrobed. With that happy thought, which he knew he would keep private in the safety of his own mind, he went back to sleep, and did not wake again until sunrise.

Chapter 17

In the morning, the mood in the camp was resolute and sour. The British commander had declined the offer of surrender, and Gabriel saw Roger speaking with great animation to Thomas, who sat in despondency at his table.

He approached the men, and Roger said, "As you may have determined for yourself, the good captain has refused our offer. He believes that our numbers are exaggerated, that his are more dedicated to their cause, and, I suppose, that he can be reinforced from Pensacola, after all. We have espied runners leaving from the west gate to the fort, beyond the range of our musketry or cannon, and can only assume that he has dispatched notices to the forces there."

Thomas said something to Roger and the ship's master replied, then saying to Gabriel, "He says that he will continue to pray for the captain to have a change of heart, but for now, he wishes only to sleep until it is all over." Thomas rose and returned to his bedroll, uncaring that the two men watched with compassion.

Roger sighed, "I suppose it can do no harm for you to hear the captain's words for yourself," and drew a copy of the captain's reply from his shirt. "Here, I'll translate it for you—the insolent dog replied in English."

He read, with an impatient tone, "Sir, I have the honor to acknowledge the receipt of your Excellency's summons to surrender immediately the fort to your Excellency's superior forces."

With a sour look, he added, "Not superior enough for him, though, it seems," and then continued reading.

"The differences of number, I am convinced, are greatly in your favor, sir, but mine are much beyond your Excellency's conception, and were I to give up this fort on your demand I should be regarded as a traitor to my King and country. My love for both, and my own honor, direct my heart to refuse surrendering this fort until I am under conviction that resistance is in vain."

Roger shook his head at the captain's obstinacy and went on, "The generosity of your Excellency's mind is well known to my brother officers and soldiers, and should it be my misfortune to be added to their number—" he snorted under his breath, "no idea what he means by that," before going on, "—a heart full of generosity and valor will ever consider brave men fighting for their country as objects of esteem and not revenge. I have the honor, et cetera, et cetera."

Gabriel frowned, his heart sinking as he realized that the British captain meant to fight it out, even if it should cost him and his entire garrison their lives. "What will it benefit them to fight to the death, when our victory is all but assured by our numbers?"

Roger shook his head sadly, answering, "I know not, but he is obviously counting on our general's good conduct, once we do prevail, with that last bit." He snorted. "The man is certainly firm in his conviction that he can somehow bring us to grief, but I do not understand the source of his confidence."

Gabriel scowled, counting off the possibilities. "It may be that he has word of some reinforcing movement that we have not yet received intelligence of, but as we know, the road overland from

Pensacola is punishingly difficult, while the seaborne access to the bay is closed at the mouth by the general's foresight."

Roger nodded, and Gabriel continued, "He may know something of the terrain that gives him hope that his force can find a way to undo our advantage of numbers, but I trust General Gálvez to have learned the lessons of his encounter at Baton Rouge, that he may apply them again in this circumstance."

Roger again nodded agreement, saying, "I have heard many who were there say that the general's strategy saved many lives on both sides, while bringing about the conclusion of the matter that would have happened had they contested it in blood and blades."

"Exactly," Gabriel replied. "That leaves us with the last possibilities, both of which are entirely possible. Either the captain of the fort intends to merely put up enough of the appearance of a fight that he can then lay down arms with his honor intact, or else he has persuaded himself that he actually holds the upper hand, and we will only be able to disabuse him of this notion by utterly destroying him and his garrison."

Roger sighed heavily, glancing over to where Thomas had wrapped himself up in his bedroll to block out the morning sunlight. "If that is the case, then our friend's sacrifices will all have been in vain."

Gabriel pursed his lips, following the ship master's gaze in the direction of the British deserter's bedroll. "How can we best help the captain to achieve the appearance of sufficient resistance, while preparing for the possibility that we will be left no option but to destroy him and his troops?"

Roger raised his eyebrows and tipped his head, saying, "I do not know the answer to that question, but I can give you every assurance that they are giving it a great deal of thought in the general's tent this morning."

He glanced again at the deserter, adding, "For his sake—and ours—I hope that they find a good answer."

By the time that the troops had all broken fast, it appeared that General Gálvez thought that he might have found an answer. The troops took advantage of the cover offered by a line of houses, and began to dig in artillery emplacements, sited to permit their crews to rain shot down within the fort, as well as to play across the face of the walls.

Even as this construction was underway, the great cannon emplaced above the fort began pounding at its walls, heedless of the musket fire from within. As at Fort Bute, Gálvez positioned his guns outside of musket range until he could get new emplacements dug in to protect them at closer positions.

Throughout the next few days, the big guns boomed in greeting across the fortification, knocking loose bricks and rattling nerves in the town. At dusk one evening, the artillery within the fort answered briefly, sending balls of pitch to burn the homes that had screened the Spanish positions. The general ordered his men to assist the residents in escaping the flames, but there was little that could be saved from the structures, and when the dawn broke, nothing remained of them but smoking skeletons.

Roger laughed at breakfast as he shared with Gabriel the correspondence that had resulted from this action. "The general, he sent a letter protesting on the behalf of the townspeople whose homes were fired, and the captain replied, suggesting a different position, which, he claims, offers a better vantage for our guns, without exposing the town to the hazards of being in between our forces."

He paused, chuckling, to mop his brow, adding, "I have to wonder if your assessment wasn't correct, and that the captain is but looking for the appearance of sufficient resistance to abandon his position with honor."

Gabriel shook his head, saying, "I shudder to think of what the delay is costing his men, though. The shots that we have been firing into the fort cannot have been to no effect whatever, and we have certainly done substantial damage already to the walls from without as well."

He gestured toward the town, where columns of smoke yet rose from the ruins. "The families driven from their homes by the very forces ostensibly placed here to protect them cannot be too kindly disposed toward the captain now, either. I should not be surprised if we were to see more deserters joining our ranks in the days to come."

Roger laughed and said, "I have my hands full translating for just the one. Are you trying to drive me to drink?"

Gabriel favored the ship's master with a weak smile, saying, "You need no encouragement to the drink, my friend, and I think that we both know that." They had shared tales of life ashore, and Gabriel had heard stories of exploits that far exceeded his own.

Changing the subject, Gabriel asked, "How much of the wall yet stands, as we face it?"

Roger nodded, pointing to Gabriel in confirmation. "You have your eye on exactly the factor which the general and his officers are most hopeful of. With good fortune and good aim, the wall should be breached in just another few days' shooting. After that," he shrugged, "it is anybody's guess how long it will take to subdue the garrison within."

Gabriel pulled Salvador's blade from its scabbard at his hip and gazed down the length of the blade. "I hope that we do not have to go to such measures, but if it is to be so, then I am ready."

The siege ground on, with the defenders lobbing well-ranged artillery out of their walls even as cannon balls and shells continued to rain within and against their walls. The points that the British had so carefully ranged, however, were those that General Gálvez had anticipated, and his forces were safely disposed elsewhere.

In contrast, however, the parts of the British fortification that the Spanish forces needed to target were not moveable, and with the continuing bombardment, they were growing less impressive than the day before.

Watching as the gun crews continued their daily target practice against the now badly tumbled-down wall of Fort Charlotte, Gabriel and Roger conversed over the periodic deep-throated boom of the cannon.

"With each passing day, and no reinforcing troops arriving from the east, the outcome of this little siege seems a little more inevitable, wouldn't you say Gabriel?"

Gabriel nodded, surveying the damage to the wall, noting where the brick facing had been blasted away, exposing the tight-packed sand and rocks within. Another cannon flew, and he watched the shot arc through the air, landing in a spray of debris. He could see that the sandy fill material within the walls was absorbing the shock of the ball without shifting very much, and wondered if the supplies that their forces had dragged to this place would, in fact, be sufficient to pierce the stout walls of the fort.

He turned back to Roger and said, "I am concerned, my

friend, that their walls will outwait our supplies of powder and shot. Might we be able to bring some other factor to bear on the defenders?" He paused for a long moment before continuing, reluctant to give voice to a thought that had occurred to him late in the night, and had been growing in his mind since.

Roger held his hands up in a gesture to convey that he had no new ideas in this regard, and Gabriel took a deep breath before saying, "Did not Thomas mention that Captain Durnford holds an estate in this town, outside of the protection of the fortifications here? I should wonder if he would continue to be so obstinate in holding his position, should that estate come to some visible grief."

Roger's eyes opened wide, and his brows raised high, as another round was fired, forcing him to wait until the din had subsided to respond. "You bring up a very fine thought, my friend. I had forgotten that detail of Thomas' narration, but you are likely correct in your assessment that it would strike at the good captain's very heart, should he see his home despoiled."

He nodded vigorously to himself, and turned to hurry away, muttering, "That'd break his will, it would, beyond anything that we've yet done here at the walls of his fort." Turning back to Gabriel, he waved and said, "I must go and share your idea with the general, and see what he thinks of it. I shall be certain to give you all credit where it is due, but I will bring this directly to his ear."

Soon after, he rushed back to Gabriel, exclaiming, "The general thinks it is a capital idea, and asked me to pick a squad to go and take care of the business at dawn. Should you like to come along?"

Gabriel nodded, his reluctance to strike directly at the personal property of an honorable enemy tempered by a desire to see the siege finish. The constant pounding and crash of the guns was enough to give most anyone a headache, and he found himself longing for the peace and quiet of a dog watch at sea, where the loudest thing was the moon sliding down below the horizon.

David joined them, too, and several other young men picked from the ranks of the militia. Roger was operating under the assumption that local militia would be more familiar with the construction—and weaknesses—of the plantation buildings. Although this assumption had little foundation in fact, none of the men chosen for the expedition were much disposed to correct it, as the mission offered them some relief from the monotony of the siege.

Roger secured a small launch for the use of the group, and brought Thomas along as well, to guide them to the captain's plantation. The British deserter had initially been cool to the idea of targeting the personal property of the fort's commander, but as he thought about it, he became more enthusiastic, to the point of urging the crew to greater exertions as they raised sails to drive the launch across the bay.

A brisk breeze had them approaching the eastern shore of the bay by mid-morning, and it was well before noon when Roger guided the prow of the launch a scraping halt on the sandy shore below the cliff where Thomas had directed him. The squad found a path to the top, and approached the plantation buildings cautiously, wary for any defense.

Like most of the habitations of the district, though, it had been evacuated as the Spanish forces had appeared in the bay, and only a handful of slaves remained on site, trying to maintain the fields and forage of the plantation.

As the squad came into the open and approached the plantation house, one of the slaves shouted out a warning, and they all ran to him, huddling under the eaves of a low barn, roofed in thatch. With a deep chuckle, Roger loaded his musket, saying to Gabriel, "Watch this."

He aimed at the roofline of the barn and fired, the sound of the shot startling the slaves into flight across the fields. The hot ball of the musket shot set the thatched roof smoldering, and, as the breeze blew across it, the dry material burst into open flame. The slave leader, who had stopped in the distance to watch, now turned and motioned to his fellows to come away with him to some other place of safety.

Gabriel grimaced at Roger, saying, "Those poor devils will be searching for a new place to sleep tonight, though it's no fault of theirs that their master has made himself the target of our attentions today."

Roger shrugged, replying, "They are but slaves, Gabriel, and they will have no trouble finding work to occupy their hands and a roof to shelter under among the neighboring plantations. Most of the places in this area are empty, in any event, so I would not spend any time worrying over the fate of a few blackbirds."

Gabriel frowned, but said nothing, instead watching as the flames spread across the roof of the barn, thick smoke beginning to billow skyward as the stores within were consumed. "Before we fire the main house, we ought to see what provisions the captain has about that might serve better in our camp than in smoke."

Roger grinned, replying, "I have had the very same thought.

Come, let us go and see."

The squad jogged together to the low structure, keeping upwind of the growing conflagration of the barn. The house was built of brick, "That will make it harder to set afire," Roger grunted to Gabriel, kicking at the whitewashed brick wall as they entered. "There is plenty to burn within, though, so let us see what may be taken away, and then be on with our work here. Follow me."

As they entered the dining room, David, behind Gabriel called out, pointing, "That is a fine set of pewterware there."

Roger nodded and motioned over one of the other men to gather up the metal dishes. "Put them outside, safely away, and let us see what else there may be. Can we find the larder?"

Gabriel said, "If this place is at all like the fine houses along the Mississippi River, the whole of the kitchen will be at a distance from the main house, so as to spare the occupants the heat of cooking during the summer."

Roger nodded again, saying "That's a sensible assumption, but let us be thorough. Thomas and David, take Humberto and Marcus, and check the bedchamber. Take any paintings, candlesticks or valuables, and put them all out with the pewter." He fixed each of the militia men with a steady gaze. "Do not think to secret anything out for your own, without you have checked with me first, understand?"

All three militia men nodded assent. He said something briefer in English to Thomas, who nodded with a smile, and the four of them moved into the other room, alert for targets of plunder. Gabriel and Roger continued to examine the front room, pointing out items for Esteban and Raul to take outdoors.

David and his companions reappeared, each carrying a

few items, and David said, "It would appear that the captain took away many of his valuables when the house was evacuated, but we did find these few things, in addition to a number of fine bed things." He quirked an eyebrow and added with a faint blush, "Most would be of no interest to us, as it appears that the captain has a young wife, and her sizes and tastes differ widely from those of a militia man."

Roger smiled at the other man's discomfiture, some of the tension of his bearing evaporating. "Very good, David." He clapped his hands and said, "Very well, let us remove ourselves from here and finish our work. Everybody out of the house, and let us take account of every soul we came here with before we commit the house to the flames."

The men filed outside, and Roger carefully counted them off before he walked over to the barn, seizing a burning timber from the flames, and threw it through the doorway of the house. The timber sat on the floor within, filling the room with smoke, but eventually flickering out without starting a wider fire.

Roger sighed and went back to the barn, this time carrying two burning brands. He walked around to the back room window and tossed one within, and threw the other onto the rooftop, before noting that it was made of inflammable tile. He sighed again, thankful that the other men had not followed him around the house, and watched in gratitude as the "fancy beddings" were evidently quite flammable.

Despite the brick walls and tile roof, within a few more minutes, thick, black smoke poured from all of the windows and doors of the building, and by the time the men had finished carting the plunder down the cliff path for loading into the launch, the roof of the house had collapsed as its timbers burned away, and the chimney had cracked and toppled.

As the group gathered at the top of the cliff face to watch the barn and house burn, David asked, "Can we go and seek out the kitchen facilities now? There may be some victuals there—" he saw Gabriel's barely-contained mirth "—that we could bring back for the benefit of all in our camp."

Roger smiled as well, and waved David on. "Go ahead," he said, "See what you can find, and if it should appear to be possible to fire that as well, make a good effort at it."

Before David could leave, though, the other militia men shot Roger questioning glances and Raul said, "May we accompany David, just in case there is too much there for him to carry back alone?"

Roger laughed aloud now and waved his hands at them all. "Yes, all of you can go. We will wait here for you, and ensure that the flames here leave no part of the estate buildings."

As the men left eagerly, chattering among themselves in speculation as to what they might find in the kitchen of a military commander and plantation owner, Roger smiled after them, his expression tinged with sadness.

He turned to Thomas and Gabriel and said, "I must confess that this wanton destruction does not bring me the joy that I had anticipated it would. It is a necessary stroke in the pursuit of this contest, but it is no happy thing to turn a man's home into ash and ruin."

Thomas looked at him in confusion, and Roger repeated himself in English. Thomas stared at the leaping flames and nodded, replying in English. Roger nodded in reply and translated for Gabriel, "He says that it will be well worth the destruction, should it bring his brother and father safely out of the fort."

Gabriel could only nod in reply, nearly mesmerized with the rising column of smoke. He wondered if the captain could see it from the fort, and turned away to look over in the direction of town, from where the low thunder of cannon fire still rolled across the bay, in counterpoint to the pops and crackles of the fires here.

From this vantage, he could see nothing of the fort across the bay, but he had little doubt that the stubborn British commander would soon learn of his latest loss, and hoped that it would help to loosen his resolve.

The breeze shifted then, and the smoke from the burning buildings swung around to where Roger and his companions stood. Roger followed Gabriel and Thomas out of the plume of smoke, and shifted to and fro for a moment, trying to get a view of the area behind the burning main house.

"I cannot see them, my friend," he said to Gabriel, a note of concern creeping into his voice. "Where could they have gone?"

Gabriel pulled himself up onto the branches of a nearby tree, gaining a higher vantage point. From there, he could see a low, undistinguished-looking structure perhaps twenty paces behind the main house, half-concealed in a small copse of trees. The smoke shifted again, and he lost sight of the building.

Frowning, he lowered himself from the branches, saying, "It looks like the kitchen is just back there. Let us go and look after their situation ourselves, but with caution. I could not see the men in the brief moment that I could see the building, but I would not leap to panic just yet."

Nonetheless, all three men found themselves crouching

instinctively as they started toward the presumptive kitchen. Their route and the shifting wind combined to bring them into another thick plume of smoke, this time from the nearly-exhausted fire in the barn. They sped up and emerged, coughing and choking, and with their eyes streaming.

Gabriel stopped abruptly at the sight that greeted them, with Thomas and Roger practically skidding to a stop beside him. The kitchen area was nestled in the shade of the trees that had interfered with Gabriel's view, and sprawled about in the clearing behind the covered cooking area were the militia men. David was nearest to them, and as they came into view, he turned his head, saying, "Eh . . . Gabriel?"

He scrambled to his feet as he took note of the building expressions of rage on Gabriel's and Roger's faces. Thomas appeared to be barely able to conceal his amusement as the events that had unfolded became clear, looking around the clearing.

Roger finally found his power of speech and asked in a low voice, filled with controlled fury, "Why did you not fire this place and return to us after you secured what plunder was available? And why did we need to come here ourselves to find you and the rest looking to all appearances as though you were ready for your *siesta?*"

David swallowed hard and looked around at the other men, who were all standing up hurriedly and brushing grass and dirt from their clothes. Finding himself representing the group single-handedly, he said, gesturing in the direction of the cooking area, "Well, you see, the blackbirds you chased off had made themselves a big pot of stew before we got here, and . . . there was no way to carry the whole pot off, so we thought to carry off just the contents, and, well, the best way to do that was . . ."

He trailed off, gesturing sheepishly at the other men, and then resting his hand on his own belly. Roger continued to glare at him, but Thomas' mirth was contagious, and Gabriel, too, was having trouble keeping a straight face. Roger whirled on them and they both composed themselves, but after a moment, his mouth quirked into a smile and he turned back to the men.

"I must commend you for your diligence in preventing any potential plunder from going to waste, but I must also observe that you have so far failed in your duty to set this place afire as well." He looked around at the cooking area and the small shed close alongside it. "Was there anything that was easily removable to the benefit of our encampment?"

"Nothing but a few implements, some of which I cannot deduce a purpose for, and others which I am certain we have in abundance. They did not seem to be keeping anything in the way of stores, but were instead gathering and slaughtering only as they needed to in order to provide for themselves."

Roger nodded and said, "Very well, I suppose that we are ready to fire this place and return to our encampment, then?"

David eagerly nodded and ran to the smoldering barn wall, where he seized a timber, and on pulling it free, found that it was but smoking. He tried a second, and then a third, and finally came upon a still-lit brand, with which he hurried back to the kitchen area. Tossing it into the shed, he stood back as the dry wooden structure quickly caught fire.

The squad stood and watched as the flames spread to the tilted roof that protected the cooking area from the rain and heat. As the fire consumed the supporting beams and trusses, the sheltering roof fell, and the group turned to leave.

As they neared the cliff path, and Roger directed the men to begin gathering the goods stacked there, Thomas seized his arm and said something in English. Roger's eyebrows went up, and he said, "Hold on a minute there, men. Thomas says that we've missed the best part here."

The two conversed in rapid-fire English, and then Roger grinned widely. Turning back to the rest of the squad, he said, "It would appear that the fine British captain has provided a hospital for the care of his men. It will be unoccupied now, naturally, as the infirmary within the fort's walls is the only surgery that they can safely gain access to. Thomas will show us the way to the hospital, and we shall fire that as well."

David and the other men grinned in reply, and they all hurried to follow Thomas as he led them past the smoking piles of rubble that marked the house, the barn and the kitchen, where several of the men took burning timbers and carried them like torches in a procession behind the British deserter.

He led them to another brick building, whitewashed to help keep it cool, and consisting of a series of rooms that each opened to the front. Roger inspected the interior rapidly, and found that it had long since been looted of anything worthwhile. Emerging from the last room at the end, he nodded to the militia men. "Burn it."

Each man with a brand chose a door, and they tossed the lot of them up into the rafters, onto the beds, and into the storage cabinets that gaped open. Again, like a recurring nightmare, smoke billowed from the windows and doors, followed by flames, and followed in due time by the sudden crack of ceiling joists as the roof sagged under its now-unsupported weight.

With a vast shower of sparks and a slow, moaning creak, the roof collapsed, falling all the way into the crater of the brick walls. For some reason, the cry of the hospital roof seemed to take all of the joy out of the day's work from everyone, and they wordlessly turned and walked back to the cliff path, where they carried down their spoils and returned to the launch for the trip back to camp.

Chapter 18

The booming of the great guns was finally silent. In its place, Gabriel could hear the sound of a rank of men around him breathing heavily, ready for the order to follow the first group of soldiers who had scrambled through the breach in the fort's thick walls.

He could hear sporadic musket fire as the defenders and invaders traded shots over the jumbled landscape of brick and rock strewn on both sides of the jagged gap in the wall before them. Too, he could hear men shouting orders to one another, words of encouragement and catcalls, in both Spanish and English.

The commander of his group gave the order, and Gabriel was surprised to realize that one of the voices raised to add to the hoarse cacophony as they charged forward was his own. The rank of militia men broke down pretty quickly into a disorganized mass, each man looking to his own footing as they ran toward the walls.

Musket fire rang out and Gabriel heard the angry buzz of a ball passing near enough to give him pause, then he shook off the fear that traveled in the shot's wake, continuing to charge forward with his fellows.

As he reached the wall, he crouched down behind a section of brick facing that sat at a crazy angle atop a slumped pile of sand. He could feel the mortar between the bricks under his fingertips as he concealed himself and pulled his gun from where he'd slung it across his shoulders. He checked the load to ensure that it was ready to fire, and quickly popped up to see what he could spot within the fort.

The effects of nearly two weeks of artillery barrages and cannon fire were everywhere to be seen. The structures within the fort were pock-marked and scored, and yet Gabriel was surprised to see that most of the buildings seemed still to be structurally sound.

The major giving them their commands before they formed up to charge had been succinct. "Shoot at anything in a red coat, and avoid shooting those on your own side. Look for the indigo-dyed kerchiefs on their arms. Stay down when you can, to avoid giving the defenders a target, but do not let fear of them make you shy. We are many; they are few. Let's drive them out, and send them back to England, where they belong."

From his position behind the bricks, Gabriel could see little in the way of good targets, but he could hear a rising tide of shouts from within, and he chanced another look up. From the window of the barracks, a defender, invisible in the shadows, waved a white banner, and Gabriel could hear more of both his fellow attackers and the defenders taking up the cry, "Parley! Parley!"

The defenders who were in positions outside of the buildings laid down their arms and stood erect, and a small detachment was dispatched from the barracks to swing open the gates to the fort. Gabriel watched, shaking his head in disbelief. So quickly, it was over?

The order was called to retreat from the fortress in order to permit the opposing commanders to meet under the flag of truce. The regulars who were spread out further inside the fortress showed the way, forming up and marching out of the opened front gates in good order. After they had exited, the militia followed their lead, under the grim gaze of several of the erstwhile defenders, who stood with their arms crossed, their thoughts unspoken but nonetheless clear.

Gabriel marched with his fellow militia members through the open gates, staring in wonder at the thickness of the walls as they passed through this intact section. He thought about what a terrible marvel it was that such a sturdy and permanent-looking edifice lay tumbled in ruins just a few dozen paces away.

Back in the siege camp, the men spoke in small groups, excited rumors flashing from one man to the next. General Gálvez and his procession marched under the white flag of truce, entering into the fort to negotiate terms of surrender with Captain Durnford.

"I have heard," said Raul with a knowing smile, "that the general and the captain knew each other long before this encounter, and that they have been exchanging friendly correspondence throughout this siege."

Gabriel nodded, saying, "I know a little of this, myself, and they certainly have a decent respect for one another. After we plundered the captain's plantation, the general returned all of the pewterware that we had carried off, and I believe that he may even have apologized for the very destruction that he himself had ordered us to visit upon the captain's holdings."

Raul shook his head, chuckling, and said, "It must be a difficult thing, having to go to war with a man whom you esteem, but who, through an accident of national origin or affiliation, you are obliged to call your enemy."

Gabriel added, "I suppose that it makes this part of the affair somewhat easier, though. I do wish that we could have settled this without the bloodshed. Do we have any accounting of our losses?"

Fernando spoke up, saying, "I heard one of the regulars who went in first saying that they lost one of their men in the initial attack through the breach, and as we marched out, I saw that the British were carrying a number of their dead—perhaps as many as a half-dozen—to a grave site just outside the walls."

He glanced around the camp and shrugged. "One soldier is not so many, when you consider how many men we placed under arms in this contest. Though their casualties were also pretty limited, our opponents lost more as a proportion of their force than did we, by far."

Gabriel interjected, "It is no wonder, then, that their captain chose surrender. He has taken enough of a bloody nose that he need report no shame to his commanders, and yet he has spared his forces further bloodshed."

He looked around intently, asking, "Has anyone seen Thomas? I wonder what word he may have had of the fate of his kin among the defenders of the fort."

David said, "Thomas was taken to the rear of the camp for the duration of the direct attack, against the possibility that he might attempt to communicate our movements or plans to those within the fort." He frowned, adding, "I do not think that he had given us any cause to doubt him, and I am sorry that he was so treated after all of his service to our side."

Gabriel nodded in agreement, but said, "I understand your feelings, David, and yet, I cannot help but remember that his reason for deserting to us was to protect his brother and father; had he seen advantage to them in communicating intelligence from our camp, I have little doubt that he would have done so without hesitation."

He looked toward the rear of the camp, where Thomas presumably was being housed. "I sincerely hope that he can soon learn good news of his family's safety. He is a decent man, and I shall be glad to have this contest of arms behind us, once the general and the captain have negotiated the terms of surrender."

He shrugged then, adding, "It is no use looking for him while Roger is with the general as a translator. Thomas may be a good man, and possessed of a sharp mind, but his tongue is hopeless at our language, and what words he has learned, I cannot understand."

David and Fernando laughed out loud at this observation, and even Raul smiled. Gabriel reflected that it felt good to laugh together again, after so many months of striving for this day. He was pleased, too, that at least so far, all of the men of the village had remained safe, as though a benevolent hand had rested between them and harm.

Gabriel declined to dwell upon it, but his mind kept returning to the late-night visit from Salvador, and he unconsciously patted the handle of the old man's dagger, where it rested safe at his belt. His thoughts strayed to Carlotta for the first time in days, and he wondered whether the protection that had shielded them to this point would continue long enough to let them return home.

His musings were interrupted by someone announcing that the general's delegation had emerged from the fort, and all watched as the white flag returned to the command tent in their encampment. An order came around that all of the attacking forces should form into their units, that the army might accept the capitulation of their vanquished foes.

Shortly thereafter, he could hear the beat of the British drummers as they sounded the surrender, and the small garrison marched out under their colors. Gabriel watched the spectacle and could not help but feel compassion for these worthy opponents, as he could see their erect postures and proud regimentation as their commander formally offered his sword to the general, and his men followed suit, stacking their arms before the assembled victors.

Once the formal ceremony was complete, the British forces were marched to the rear of the encampment as prisoners. Curious as to the fate of Thomas' family, Gabriel made his way to where they busied themselves with building shelter and preparing for the first night of their defeat. Roger, too, was there, providing translation between the British officers and their Spanish captors.

When he saw Gabriel, his face lit up in a wide smile, and he greeted his friend in a rapid stream of English. He noted the confusion on Gabriel's face and quickly switched to Spanish. "I am sorry, my friend, I have been speaking English so much today that it is difficult to break the habit. We are victorious, and the prisoners have given us their parole for the next eighteen months, so we have nothing to fear from these wretches."

Gabriel raised a hand, smiling, and interrupted, "I did not expect that we had any reason to fear that they might strike at us again after their defeat. I was come here to learn the fate of Thomas' brother and father."

Roger looked thunderstruck and replied, "In all of the momentous events of the day, I had forgotten entirely about our poor friend Thomas. Let us go and find him, and aid him in seeking his family."

He shouted out a couple more comments in English to the prisoners' officers, who each nodded grimly in reply. Clapping Gabriel on the back, he asked, "Do you know where they held Thomas for the duration of the battle?"

Gabriel nodded and led the ship's master away, saying, "I should pray that his guards have given him some reason to hope. Those I have spoken to have said that the losses on both sides were very light, and so there is every reason to believe that his kin will have survived the battle."

Coming to a stop before an enclosed tent, he said to the guard, "We are here to speak with Thomas, if you please."

The guard looked at both men and asked Roger, "You are the general's translator, are you not?"

Roger bowed his head modestly and said, "I have assisted the general with certain documents and conversations, yes. We are here on a mission of mercy today, however."

The guard pondered for a moment, and then nodded and said, "You may speak to him, then. Do you suppose that we can free him from his detention, now that there is no danger that he could be of aid to the British garrison?"

Roger smiled and replied, "I fully expect so, though we will wait for the general's word, to be sure. Thank you kindly; I don't anticipate that we'll be long."

The guard pulled aside the flap and the two ducked into the tent. Once Gabriel's eyes had adjusted to the gloom within, he could see Thomas sitting on a low bench along the back of the tent. He looked up from the letter he was writing and smiled at the pair.

Roger greeted him, and asked him something in English.

Thomas nodded and replied, gesturing at the paper before him. Roger explained to Gabriel, "I just asked if he had heard the news of the fall of the fort, and he said that he had, and he is preparing a letter for his father and brother."

Thomas asked Roger something in turn, and Roger nodded seriously and replied. "He would like for us to carry the letter for him to the prisoners, and seek his family among them. I'll have to explain to him that I must read the letter to ensure that it contains no intelligence of military value, but I believe that we can transmit this correspondence without concern."

He spoke to Thomas again, explaining the conditions, and the British deserter nodded in acceptance. He made another comment, and Roger smiled in reply. "He says that he has been thinking about what this letter ought to say ever since he entered our camp, these several weeks ago."

Gabriel shook his head in sympathy. "I can only imagine that this is a difficult letter to pen. His family may think ill of him, and yet he is to explain to them the sacrifices that he has made on their behalf. I can only hope that they receive word of him with joy and excitement."

With satisfied grunt to himself, Thomas finished re-reading the letter and held it out for Roger's inspection, waving it slightly in the air to dry the ink and avoid smudges. Roger took it carefully by the edge and translated it aloud for Gabriel.

"My dear brother and esteemed father, I write this to you with hopeful anticipation for your preservation through the Spanish attack upon the fort which has lately come to the sad, but inevitable conclusion of our downfall."

Roger glanced up with an apologetic expression to Thomas

and the British deserter waved dismissively and motioned for him to continue reading.

"I give you the joy of knowing that I am unharmed, through circumstances both strange and potentially shameful, and I eagerly anticipate having the opportunity to explain myself to you both, and beg your forgiveness for any perception of disloyalty as I acted in what I felt to be the best interests of your safety." Gabriel raised an eyebrow, looking at Roger with a small shake of his head. It seemed unfortunate to him that Thomas should have to seek pardon for trying to protect his family.

"I am your most affectionate and loving son and brother, Thomas Ward."

Roger lowered the page and nodded to Thomas, and then folded the page. "It is completely innocent of anything that might be of any military use at all, and merely tells his father and brother that he is safe, that he is nearby, and that they will soon be reunited."

He chuckled to himself and said, "Captain Durnford wrote a letter to his superiors in Pensacola to inform them of his surrender. The general had me read it, like this letter, to ensure that it did not reveal information that might prove helpful to the forces there, and I was struck by his concern that the commander in Pensacola would reassure his wife that he was unharmed, and would soon be released on parole."

Shaking his head and smiling, he concluded, "It just touches my heart to see that these men, so different in station and in their current disposition, should share the same first concern." Tapping the letter on the palm of his opposite hand, he said, "Well, let us go and secure permission to bring this letter to the prisoners of war and seek out Thomas' father or brother."

Gabriel crossed himself and said, "I only pray that they are among the unhurt in their camp, and that they receive this letter in good health and good spirits."

Holding the tent flap open for Gabriel, Roger said, "I join you most fervently in those prayers, my friend." He turned back to the dark interior and said something to Thomas, who answered briefly, and Roger let the flap fall shut.

Nodding to Gabriel, Roger said, "Should you like to accompany me to the command tent, that we may quickly have the letter's contents scrutinized, and then bring it to Thomas' family without delay?"

"Certainly," replied Gabriel. "I am eager to meet Thomas' father, and to share the news of his son's safety with him."

In short order, they'd presented the letter to a junior officer, Roger had described its content, and the officer had handed it back, with a wave of his hand. "Deliver this letter to whomever you wish," he said, clearly concerned about other matters.

Roger and Gabriel escaped the command tent and made their way to the prisoner of war section of the encampment. After explaining themselves to the guards, they approached a British soldier, and Roger asked him where to find Jacob or Alexander Ward, Thomas' brother and father.

The soldier looked at Roger with a mixture of suspicion and resentment, and then pointed at one of the temporary shelters the prisoners had set up for themselves. He turned away from the two men brusquely, and Roger shrugged, leading the way to the shelter the soldier had indicated.

When they arrived, there was no question as to which men

they sought. The family resemblance to Thomas' features was striking in both father and son as they crouched, working together at bracing one of the supporting poles of the shelter.

Roger approached the elder of the pair and asked if he were Alexander Ward. The man looked up at Roger, startled both to hear his name and to hear the ship's master addressing him in English, and when he'd regained his composure, he stood and nodded.

Roger smiled at him and drew the letter from within his shirt, presenting it to Alexander without comment. The British soldier slowly opened the folded paper, his brows beetled in incomprehension until he saw the handwriting on the page. He gave an involuntary gasp and covered his mouth in disbelief, his eyes racing over the words of the missive.

His other son approached at the sound of his father's shout, and as he peered over the older man's shoulder, his eyebrows lifted into his shaggy hair. He reached over his father's shoulder and placed a finger on the letter, tracing along the words as he more slowly read them.

Gabriel took the opportunity of both men's absorption in the letter to examine them more closely than might have otherwise been considered necessarily polite. Beyond the obvious similarities in their builds and facial structures, he could see that these men had been ill-fed for some time, as their cheekbones stood out sharply. They looked weary, their eyes hung with dark circles about them, and their eyelids loose and half-closed as they read.

It was clear that whatever the difficulties of the journey to this place and the hard work of conducting a siege and charge, these were as nothing in comparison to the stress and privations of living under that siege for several weeks, hemmed in closely within a fort already overflowing with those taking refuge from the surrounding town.

Thomas' father finished reading his letter first, and handed it entirely over to Jacob. He turned away from Roger and Gabriel for a moment, seeking to compose himself before he addressed them. When he turned back, he asked Roger a lengthy and sternly worded question. Roger translated for Gabriel, "He wants a complete accounting of his son's activities since he slipped out of the British cordon upon our approach."

Shaking his head in negation, he answered the man, explaining to Gabriel, "I have told him that I will leave that to Thomas to relate, as it is hardly my place to speak for his son in so fraught a matter."

Jacob finished the letter and quietly handed it back to his father. Roger asked Alexander, translating for Gabriel, "Should you like for me to ask whether I may bring Thomas here, so that you can speak to him yourself, or would you prefer that I carry a letter back to your son?"

The older man pondered for a moment, and then came to a decision. He spoke in rapid, clipped words, and Roger nodded somberly before answering. Turning to Gabriel, he said, "He asks that we leave him in peace for an hour to consider his son's letter, and then return for his answer. I believe that we may profitably pass that time in securing permission so that Thomas can be released to come here."

He turned back to the two British soldiers and bowed slightly in respect as he bade them farewell. He then turned and led Gabriel back out of the prisoner's area and back toward the command tent.

Before they reached it, though, he stopped and said to Gabriel, "I know not whether he will see his son. It is impossible to know what they were told of his actions or fate, but it cannot have any effect but to disquiet him to have Spanish militia men come into their camp bearing word from him. Alexander is anything but a fool, and it cannot be far from his mind that his son's presence here must indicate some treachery on his part."

Roger sighed, turning back toward the command tent. "Of course, the fact that we have offered to conduct his son to him and conveyed Thomas' letter has doubtless already informed Alexander that his son is comfortably in our company. I only hope that he reads closely his son's plea for a chance to explain in detail the reasons that impelled him to his difficult course of action."

They reached the command tent and Gabriel gave Roger a wan smile. "If nothing else, we can give Thomas the assurance that his actions were not in vain, and that his kin were preserved through the fall of the garrison."

Roger nodded, and the two men entered the tent, where they sought out the same officer who had approved the letter. The man threw his hands up in frustration. "It matters not to me. We are consumed with the question of how to conduct over three hundreds of British prisoners of war to another British town, without setting them down in a place close enough by here to tempt them to break their parole to us."

He waved his hands at Roger and Gabriel, urging them out of the tent. "Go, do as you will with this man. He is of no further concern to me, unless he should be considered as one of the prisoners of war."

"I shall need a written order for the guards who are ensuring his quarantine from the prisoners of war," Roger persisted, and the officer rolled his eyes and scribbled out a pass for them.

Dipping his head in gratitude, Roger said, "I wish you good fortune in accommodating our British friends. If I may be of service to you in this matter, please do not hesitate to send for me." The officer grunted in reply and turned away, a scowl marking his face.

"I do not believe that I need look for his call," Roger remarked to Gabriel as they exited the tent, and Gabriel gave him a sideways smile.

"I believe that we are safe from any duty to him, yes. Let us go and share with Thomas the happy news that his kin are safe and sound. We can bring him with us when we go to speak again with his father, and so save ourselves much tramping back and forth across the camp."

Roger nodded and grinned at the world around him as they set off. "It is a happy thing to be bringing glad tidings, instead of the sorry news of yet another day of bombardment, preparations for extending the siege and so on."

Gabriel nodded in turn, and they walked purposefully together to the tent where Thomas remained in isolation. Roger handed the guard the pass that the officer had written for him, and the guard grinned, relaxing. "Perhaps I can go catch some sleep," he said. Then, with a frown, he added, "Of course, knowing my sergeant, there will be some other, even more rigorous duty that must be attended to."

Grumbling good-naturedly to himself, the guard walked away, turning to wave farewell, and saying, "He's all yours, boys."

Gabriel pulled aside the tent flap and again the two men

entered into the gloom. Neither of them could restrain the wide smiles that broke upon their faces when Thomas looked up at them with a questioning glance.

Roger nodded and spoke to him in English. Thomas stood and said a brief prayer of thanksgiving, his face tilted to the heavens, and then stepped forward to embrace each man in turn. He asked Roger a quick question, to which Roger nodded and gave a brief answer, which turned Thomas' expression grim and unhappy.

"He wishes to see them, naturally. I explained that his father is examining his feelings before we are to present him to them, and that it seemed that Alexander was harboring some ill will toward him for his desertion, no matter the worthiness of his reasons."

He shrugged. "It is as it is now, and fretting over what may be without knowing is a fool's errand. Let us go and raise the dice cup and see what fate has wrought."

Motioning to the entrance, he led the way as all three men exited the tent. Upon their arrival at the shelter where the Wards had been, he held up a hand to direct Thomas and Gabriel to stay outside while he spoke to Alexander.

Gabriel smiled at Thomas and crossed himself, praying that Alexander would at least hear Thomas out, and would not condemn the man, with his story unheard. From where they stood, they could hear Alexander's voice through the thin walls of the shelter, raised slightly, as if he were making an objection to something that Roger had said.

In a moment, Roger came out, shaking his head. "A most stubborn man," he said to Gabriel in Spanish, and then spoke to Thomas in English. Thomas nodded and walked into the shelter, the other two men following behind him.

Within the shelter, Alexander stood, looking sternly at Thomas. In the corner, his brother Jacob was much less subdued in his reaction to seeing Thomas for the first time in over a month. His expression was one of unrestrained joy, and it was clear that only a glare from Alexander held him back from rushing over to greet Thomas.

Alexander braced Thomas with a pointed question, which Thomas answered in quiet but urgent tones. Roger rushed to translate quietly for Gabriel's benefit, "How is it that my son is first listed as absent from the fort, then is said to be a traitor, and now stands before me as though nothing at all has happened?"

"Father, I abandoned a hopeless cause not to betray you, but to do what I could to ensure your safety."

Alexander snorted and Roger translated as Thomas continued, "I believed that by providing intelligence to our attackers, I could help to bring about a swift conclusion to the matter, keeping bloodshed to a minimum, and permitting all to claim the honor of having striven as hard as they could for the preservation of our position here in Mobile."

Alexander retorted angrily, "Do you expect me to believe that you took it upon yourself to assume the burden of dishonorable deeds, that the rest of us might retain our honor? It appears to me that your own safety was greatly assured by your actions, while ours was not greatly influenced one way or the other."

Thomas shot back, "Do you not think that these Spanish barbarians were capable of massacring our entire garrison, should we have resisted more forcefully?" He glanced over to Roger and Gabriel then, coloring slightly at the reproachful look that the ship's master gave him.

Alexander followed his glance and spoke to Roger with an ingratiating tone. He translated for Gabriel, "Do not take offense at my son's ill-thought words. He is seeking to rationalize his cowardice, and the knowledge that he holds a weak position makes him forget his manners in speaking of our gracious hosts."

Thomas interrupted, and the two spoke back and forth too rapidly for Roger to keep up. He leaned over to Gabriel and said, "In truth, had the captain demanded of his men that they fight to their last, the general would have obliged their desire for destruction." He tipped his head at the two men, saying, "They are now engaged in a heated discussion of the proper forms of rhetoric and the finer points of martial courtesy. I believe that it is appropriate for us to withdraw at this time."

Gabriel nodded in agreement, and they quietly excused themselves, dipping their heads to Jacob, who gave them a look of gratitude, even as he rolled his eyes at his brother and father. Roger and Gabriel shared a quick smile and walked away from the shelter.

As they reached their own section of the encampment, Roger looked over to Gabriel and quipped, "I am always glad to be a party to a happy reunion." Gabriel snorted in a quick laugh, and they parted ways at his tent.

Chapter 19

It was comforting to feel the deck of a ship move beneath his feet again, and to smell the fresh salt air. As he leaned against the railing of his ship, Gabriel's only disappointment was that they were sailing not westward to bring the militia home, but for Havana, where General Gálvez planned to gather his forces for the invasion of Pensacola.

Roger swung up onto deck from below, ebullient as usual. "Feels good to be free of land again, doesn't it, my friend?"

Gabriel turned and smiled at the ship's master, whose cheerfulness was contagious. "I was just thinking that I should like to be seeing a particular stretch of land again soon, but yes, it is simpler here, in many respects."

"Thinking about that widow again, are you?"

Gabriel shrugged slightly and turned back into the breeze, looking out over the rolling waves of the ocean.

Roger clapped him on the shoulder and said, "There are some fine girls in Havana who might help you to forget about her, if we're there long enough, and not on our way straight off to war again."

Gabriel turned back to face Roger, giving him a sour look before asking, "Have you seen the defenses at Pensacola yourself?"

"No, I have not had that pleasure, but it will be a tough nut to crack, in comparison to Fort Charlotte."

Gabriel corrected him, "Fort Carlotta, now." His heart lurched at speaking the name, which Gálvez had insisted upon applying to the restored fortifications, and he shook his head in reproach to himself. Gálvez had certainly not known the import of that name to the militia men from the little settlement, nor to the displaced sailor who'd accompanied them.

Roger laughed and said, "Yes, of course. In any event, I know that General Gálvez sent a spy to Pensacola last year, but I have heard stories from a number of people that the commander there, General Campbell, has been squawking for help ever since Baton Rouge, and I do not doubt that he has made improvements in that time."

He leaned on the railing beside Gabriel and continued, "There will be more men, better armaments, better fortifications and they'll be more wary of our general, to boot. We'll not be rolling over this place so easily."

Gabriel looked into the blue waves, looking for wisdom or reassurance there. The water, though it chuckled and splashed cheerfully past the sides of the ship, had nothing substantive to say, and he turned back to Roger. "I trust the general's leadership, my friend. He has brought us through challenges that might have daunted many men. When he was outnumbered, he made use of his force's nimbleness. When we held the advantage in numbers, but found himself ill-positioned, he overcame the weakness of our position by making sharp use of the size of our army."

He nodded to himself and to the ocean. "He will find a way to apply his strengths against the enemy's weakness, and I like our chances to finally drive the English out of West-Florida entirely."

Roger wore a thoughtful expression as he said, almost more to himself than in reply to Gabriel, "And is the Spanish King liable to be a better manager of this rich land than has been mad George?" He frowned, as though he regretted speaking aloud, and turned away, saying, "I am on watch at the bell, and I had best attend to my preparations."

Gabriel thought about what might be the answer to his friend's musings. He honored King Carlos, and even felt respect for the man's achievements since he had taken the throne. However, Spain was far away, and her colonies in the new world did not come before the sovereign's daily concerns very often. Likewise, the King had hardly had any effect on Gabriel's life before he was called upon to serve in this war, fighting against another distant king.

Roger had owed fealty to the King of England, and had turned his back on that obligation, though Gabriel had never had reason to believe that it was with any conscious intent. Now, though, he wondered. He'd heard others refer to "Mad George of England," but he'd always dismissed it as the sort of talk one hears about the leader of the enemy. He resolved to ask Roger about his former king another time, perhaps after he'd had a double ration of rum to loosen his tongue.

Looking about the horizon, he felt a sense of disquiet, and had to think hard about its source, until he realized how rarely he'd sailed out of sight of land before. To be sure, there were the sails of the fleet, arrayed in good order along the path of their route, but other than that, the sea was empty. His unease was, he realized, almost childish, like a boy hanging on his mother's apron strings. He laughed at himself and went below deck to attend to his duties there.

A few days later, the fleet sailed into the great harbor at Havana, through narrows guarded on each side by tidy but stout fortresses. They then passed the imposing bulk of a fortification that dwarfed any that Gabriel had ever before laid eyes on.

Roger called out from the wheel of the ship, "It is called *la Cabaña*, and I've heard that it is the biggest fort Spain has built anywhere."

The crenelated wall went on and on, with the hungry maw of one gun after another gaping out over the entrance to the bay. Men hailed the fleet from the tops of the wall, and signal guns spoke from the fort and from the flagship, doing the customary honors to one another.

Roger called out again, "After we lost and regained Havana, almost a score of years ago now, the King resolved never to lose this place again." He laughed, adding, "After all, the last time, it cost him all of Florida to get this one city back. Not a bad trade, mind you, but a costly one, to be sure."

He pointed to the shore opposite the fort, where the city proper clustered along neatly laid-out streets. "The fort is wondrous, to be sure, but over there, now that's a place of wonder indeed." He raised his eyebrows and gestured as though he were lifting a glass to his mouth. "Rum, my friend, the like of which you have never tasted, and will never taste again."

Gabriel laughed in reply, saying, "It is but a drink for setting my mind at ease before I retire for the night, and I am not so deeply in its thrall that I must compare different sorts. Rum is rum—it all comes from cane, and it all goes to ruin."

Roger looked at him reprovingly. "Do not ever let them

hear you say such a thing in this city," he said. "They will give you an education the like of which it will take you a week of nights to fully recover from."

Gabriel shook his head, still chuckling. "I will leave the lessons for your benefit, my friend, and will not waste them on my poor palate."

Roger waved his hand as though dismissing a naughty schoolboy. "Very well, but there are other pleasures to be found here as well."

Gabriel shook his head, a slow smile on his face. "You know my interests lie elsewhere on this Spanish lake, my friend. I am no monk, but I am also no longer a cabin boy. I will get to know this city while the general makes his preparations for the strike at Pensacola, but I do not intend to behave shamefully."

Laughing, Roger fired back, "Ah, but with the action at Pensacola looming, if you were to fall there, would you want your final thought to be, 'O, but I wish I had tasted the fruits of Havana,' or would you rather reflect on your happy misbehavior here? I warn you, Gabriel, there is no bitterer draught than regret."

"I shall take that chance, Roger, for I would rather not live a life of regret for the acts that I did commit here." He grinned, and then his expression shifted rapidly as he pointed, his mouth agape. "Is that a real *catedral*? I had never hoped to lay eyes on the like of that in this life."

Visible inland from the bay, though set low before the gentle slope that rose behind it, the cathedral's twin towers rose high above the city, with a façade far more detailed and ornate than any work even in the great town of New Orleans. As their ship passed the end of the great fort on the other side of the bay, the bells for evening prayer pealed out from where they swung in one of the towers, and Gabriel crossed himself.

Roger noticed this and raised an eyebrow at him. "Not a monk, eh?" He raised his hands, smiling. "It is your life, live it as you please. There will be more rum and more girls for me if you are spending your time gaping in awe at the cathedral and saying your rosary."

Gabriel scowled in mock annoyance, and then laughed. "I do not look forward to carrying you back on board for dosing by the surgeon for whatever dread ailment you suffer after your time ashore. Though you mock me now, you will depend upon me in your time."

Once ashore, though, the lighthearted mood that had prevailed as they arrived was gone, erased by the intelligence that awaited them and General Gálvez' order that the men remain at readiness to sail, just as soon as the additional forces he had requested were gathered. Roger returned to the ship with what details were known outside the lofty reaches of the military command.

"As we had heard before we sailed, the British have gotten word of General Gálvez' successes in Baton Rouge and Mobile, and they have sent a great many ships and several full regiments of the regular army. In addition, they have been augmented with loyalist militias, and even several thousands of the Indians of the region have been induced to come to their aid in Pensacola."

Gabriel nodded, saying, "This is not news, however. What is there that so concerns the general that he does not grant us leave to go ashore for more than a few hours' time?"

"The English are not the only ones who have sent for reinforcements, and it sounds likely that the general has received word that his are near at hand, so that they need not do more than merely touch here at Havana, taking on such stores as they have consumed, and we can then set out without delay for the attempt on Pensacola."

Gabriel pursed his lips, nodding. "Would that we had time to explore what parts of this city most interested us each, but I am even more eager for this entire enterprise to be complete, that we may return to our homes and resume the lives that we pursued before the needs of kings upended everything."

Roger smiled and shook his head, gazing out over the city, just out of reach beyond the ropes that held their ship to its anchorage. "Remember, my friend, what I said of regret, and let us hope that things work out as you have hoped."

Chapter 20

It was a splendid thing, Gabriel decided, to be part of a great invasion fleet sailing out of harbor to do the work of God. The Admiral, who had summoned the captains of all the ships together the prior night, had sent up the signal to weigh anchors at morning's first light, and so numerous were the ships of the fleet that it took all day, and well past sundown, for the last of them to tack out of the great harbor of Havana through *la Canal de Entrada*, and out into the open water of the Gulf beyond.

Gabriel's old friend Captain Batista had once again gained his own command, one of the score and a dozen of troop carriers that sailed in the convoy, much like the one on which Roger and Gabriel had sailed into Havana, and on which they would sail out as well. Although Gabriel had been unable to secure assignment to his former captain's ship, he had sent a message of congratulations, and regret that the chances of military service had not brought them back together.

Gabriel's ship had passed under the watchful guns of *la Cabaña* as the deepening light of the setting sun painted the walls of the fort in gold and flame. Looking back at the city, Gabriel could see only the spires of the cathedral, outlined in sharp contrast to the sunset behind. He crossed himself and said a brief prayer to San Miguel before going below to attend to his duties in the hold.

The next morning, as he moved about the ship at his tasks,

Gabriel saw dozens of the ships of the fleet stood in fine order, but merely creeping northward, under reefed sails. He stopped by Roger's post to inquire as to the reason for their slowed progress, and the ship's master replied with a scowl, "We have not yet caught sight of the dozen and more ships that came out of Havana after darkness fell last night, and the Admiral is hoping to bring the fleet together as one before we set off for Pensacola."

He waved his hand in the direction of the hazily visible horizon and said, "They have probably gotten ahead of us in the night, having failed to make the lights of the trailing end of the fleet as they came out behind us." He shrugged. "Before much longer, we will get underway without them, if I don't miss my guess, and hope to encounter them as we go, that we may arrive as a single hammer blow upon the defenses at Pensacola."

Gabriel nodded, and indeed, he saw signal flags flash out along the squadron as the flagship's sails were unfurled and filled with the morning breeze, and the rest of the ships in the line followed suit. Hurrying back to his duties, he was glad for every mile that passed beneath the bow of his ship, for though it might bring him further from the village, it brought him closer to returning.

By midday, the breeze had freshened and the light scud of clouds that had accompanied them out of Havana darkened into heavier, more menacing overcast, and Gabriel found himself on deck at every opportunity, nervously watching the skies. Too often, he had seen a fine morning of sailing turn into a terrible night under similar circumstances.

Such was to be the case this night, it seemed. The crew went through the well-practiced routine of taking in the sails one by one, until by the time dark had fallen, the little ship proceeded under no more than a closely reefed foresail, more to maintain her heading than to gain speed. Absolute torrents of rain screamed out of the sky, and the captain ordered the crew to work one of the pumps after Gabriel reported two feet of water in the hold.

Throughout the night, the seas increased in their ferocity, pitching the ship about in a terrible fashion. The troops aboard suffered the worst for the violence of the storm, and the ship's erstwhile doctor—appointed on the strength of his experience as a chirougen's assistant—was in keen demand as one man after another was dashed from his feet or tossed from his hammock, with injuries ranging from a shattered leg to any sort of contusion one might care to imagine.

When the morning dawned, only one other ship of the convoy could even be made out through the squalls, and her condition was shocking to behold. Her mainsprint and foremast had been carried away in the night, and she appeared to be riding at a list, as though the crew had yet to cut away all of the wrecked parts, leaving them dragging by the rigging that had held them in place.

As yet another torrential squall hid their sister ship, Gabriel could see men working heroically with axes and knives, slicing away the wounded parts of their ship that what remained might weather whatever the storm did to her next, and he murmured a quick prayer for their sakes.

His own little ship shuddered as it hit a wave at a bad angle, and not long after, Gabriel had to report to the captain that the depth of the water in the hold was still increasing slowly, despite the labors of the men on the pump. The man acknowledged Gabriel's report with a curt nod, and then turned away to order that the other pumps be manned and worked.

Gabriel returned below, and though he scarcely could admit it to himself, he was glad for the respite from the rain and the wind that he found there. Shifting cargo about in the hold to protect from the damp what needed protecting, while ensuring that the troops aboard did not suffer more than could be avoided, took up most of his attention, and he was surprised when the bells sounded that told him that he'd been at it for most of two watches without relief.

He greeted his earnest young assistant with relief as the younger man relayed the captain's order to get some rest if possible. Conveying the current state of affairs to his assistant, he secured himself in his hammock and slept, though it was hard to call it rest. Between the wild movement of the ship, controlled though it was under Roger's sure and competent hand, and the nightmares engendered by the sounds and sensations of the storm's fury, Gabriel spent his time off watch alternating between lying awake in worry and fitfully dreaming in terror.

Waking with the bells declaring his watch resumed, Gabriel checked the hold as he relieved his assistant, and was glad to report to the captain that the efforts of the crews on the pumps had borne fruit through the day. The hold was awash with no more than a foot of water, barely enough to be concerned about. The captain released all but one of the pump crews back to their other duties, or to rest belowdecks. Many of the men on the pumps had been drawn from the ranks of the troops aboard, unused to the sort of unceasing toil that naval service imposed. Gabriel could feel their gratitude as an almost palpable thing as they streamed past to the relative dry comfort of their hammocks.

As he emerged into the storm again, Gabriel noted that Roger was off watch. Shouting to be heard above the storm, he asked the man at the wheel, "How do we fare?"

He replied with a grimace and a shrug, shouting back, "The master is below, as he was hit on his watch by a block falling from the shredded rigging above. He refused to step away until the bell rang, but what I've heard from those who witnessed the incident, he is fortunate indeed to have suffered no more than a nasty bruise on his shoulder." Gabriel nodded and grimaced in reply, again murmured a prayer for the safety of his friends and shipmates, as he moved to attend to his duties on the deck.

Throughout the long hours of his watch, the storm raged, now intensifying, then abating for a bit, before settling back to the furious task of tearing the ship apart. Without the guidance of the bells of the watch, it would have been difficult to tell day from night, so dark were the clouds overhead.

Gabriel was belowdecks, re-checking that the heavier cargo was still secure, when the mainmast succumbed, caught by a vicious gust of wind just as the momentum of the pitching ship snapped it in the opposite direction. He felt the deck under his feet jump as he heard the timbers crack and part overhead.

After endless moments of confused noise above, the motion of the ship before the wind shifted suddenly, and Gabriel could tell even without seeing it with his eyes that a fatal disaster had overtaken the ship. By the new list of the deck below him, and the sudden sluggishness of its pitching, he guessed that the wrecked mast had fallen to port and was now hanging over the side by what rigging had failed to part as it toppled, its bulk impeding the ship's movement through the water and dragging it in a great arc upon the mountainous waves.

Leaping up the nearest companionway, he paused to grab an axe and emerged on deck to find a scene of unimaginable ruin and chaos. The downpour was so heavy that it was almost impossible to see even the fore end of the ship from where he'd emerged at aft, and rigging lay wildly tangled all about the deck. It was difficult at first to get his bearings, as the familiar waypoints of mast and rigging were all swept away and replaced with a jungle of wreckage and flying water.

Without waiting for orders, Gabriel sprang into action, guided almost by instinct as he swung his axe again and again to slice hempen lines stretched haphazardly where they did not belong, while sparing those that still served their purpose. Everywhere that the waves had yet to scour bare, splinters and beams of wood lay about, wrapped without reason with ropes and the remains of sail and other gear.

As he worked his way forward, clearing away the wreck one arduous pace along the deck at a time, Gabriel saw with a moment of saddened shock that the captain lay lifeless under the broken mast, struck down by a caprice of the wind and sea. There was no time to reflect on the loss, though, as he could feel the ship being dragged by the wreckage to a heading where it could not meet the sea properly, and would be subject to being rolled and sunk without any regard for the struggles or cares of its crew.

His arm rose again and again, and he could see other men working on different areas of the wreckage, each cutting away in moments the work of days of patient knotting and laying-out of rope and wood. As the stretch of deck before him was cleared by a wave breaking over the side, Gabriel clutched a taut line to avoid joining the flotsam overboard, and as soon as the water receded, he released the line, assessed it as being out of place, and sliced it with his axe.

With a great groan, the mast shifted across the deck where it lay, its top end tilted crazily into the water at the port side of the ship. A few more ropes parted, and it lifted entirely off the deck and started to slide over the side, before it was stopped by just a small tangle of rigging nearby where Gabriel panted, feeling as though he were breathing more spray than air. His arm rose, the axe sliced through the twisted ropes, and the ship leapt free of the wrecked mast.

Through the downpour, Gabriel could see Roger back at his position at the wheel, frenetically bringing the ship about to again face the roll of the seas in relative safety. Skillfully adjusting to the new thrust of the remaining bare masts before the driving wind, the ship's master brought the wheel about to the ideal bearing for the seas as they were, and then turned to lift a hand in gratitude to Gabriel.

As he raised his axe in a replying salute, Gabriel heard another sharp crack overhead. He glanced up, assuring himself that the portion of a cross mast falling from the mizzen was not going to strike him down, and grinned back at Roger. He did not see the line of twisted hemp that flew through the air from behind him, driven by the gale. Like a thing alive, it whipped about to wrap his raised axe and arm. As the heavy piece of wooden gear to which it was secured to flew over the starboard side, Gabriel was yanked entirely off his feet, emitting a hoarse shout of surprise.

He heard the bones of his arm snapping and grinding and pain stabbed up his arm. He could feel himself being dragged across the planking of the deck, and desperately struggled to free his hand from the accursed rope, to no avail. The axe fell from the insensate fingers of his shattered arm, even as he scrabbled at the deck with his other hand. Gabriel could see the side of the ship approaching inexorably, the cutwater carried away already, and nothing between himself and a return to the watery death he had cheated so many months before.

The howl of the wind sounded almost like a voice, and as his axe slid over the side and fell away into the water below, Gabriel would ever after swear that he heard Salvador shout a single word: "Knife."

He reached to his belt, where Carlotta's gift was still safely in its scabbard, and whipped the knife out, bringing it in a smooth arc over his head to where the line was pulled tight against the side of the ship. He saw the wild and ravenous sea below, and watched, as though time slowed down, as the blade found the line that was trying so hard to pull him down, and sliced through it as though it were no more than butter.

Released from the pull of the line, he sprang back from the edge of the deck, scrambling away until he encountered the railing that surrounded the companionway opening, his arm a single mass of agony tucked instinctively to his side. He clung gratefully, tightly, to the railing for several long moments, gasping for breath and feeling his heart leap within his chest.

As he returned to his senses, he looked in wonder at the blade in his hand, and slowly, almost reverently, returned it to its scabbard, mindless for a moment of the spray and noise and motion of the deck still plunging about beneath him. He thought only of the fine, strong hand that had placed this instrument of salvation into his hands, and the inexplicable strength that had again come to his aid.

Chapter 21

The mood that carried Gabriel through the entrance to Havana Bay the second time was considerably less buoyant than on the first time. His ship was not entering proudly, as part of a gathering invasion force, but was scarcely limping in, with jury-rigged masts and tattered sails.

This time, too, he had the weight of command upon his shoulders. With the death of the ship's captain, the crew had turned to the first mate, but a festering broken thigh had carried off that officer inside of a week after the storm's passage, and Gabriel found himself thrust into the role of making wearying decisions that would decide the fates of all aboard.

His own injuries were less grave, but his arm remained bound tightly to his side. The ship's doctor had examined it, the smell of rum heavy on his breath, and had shaken his head sadly as his fingers moved over the broken and twisted arm. Gabriel suppressed the urge to cry out as the man's fingers probed at a particularly painful spot, and the doctor pulled his hand away, saying, "I have not the skill to set these breaks, sir. Keep it bound up, and I can give you a physic that should help the bones knit, but I cannot restore your arm."

His eyes narrowing at the sight of *la Cabaña's* flags, Gabriel gave the order for the routine signal cannon, and sighed inwardly. He was thankful for the advice and experience that his old friend

Roger had been able to offer him, but in the end, it had been his decision to bring the ship back to Havana, and he could only hope that his superiors would agree that he'd given the right command under the circumstances.

There had been several desperate days following the storm's abatement when he was unsure whether they would make it back to any dry land at all. The little ship had not been made for the kind of abuse it had taken under the crashing waves and tearing winds of the storm, and she had taken on water at a prodigious rate, a rate that only slowed when the crew used the desperate expedient of wrapping the leakiest part of the hull closely with a sail.

Gabriel had still been driven to ordering nearly constant watches on all pumps, wearing the men to the ragged edge of complete exhaustion to keep water pouring over the sides as they slowly sailed on. Throughout the ordeal, Gabriel had needed to maintain the fiction that he was capable and knowledgeable enough to command the crew, all the while taking meals with Roger in the privacy of the captain's cabin, where they could talk in complete frankness.

Along with the unsought thrill of his own first command, Gabriel had the additional burden of grief. The first ship of the scattered squadron that they'd come near enough to that they could exchange signal flags had reported the loss of many ships of the fleet, including that of his old friend Captain Batista.

Manuel's little troopship had been seen foundering low in the water in the heavy seas of the first day of the storm, completely dismasted, and Gabriel knew in his heart that there was no hope that even the quick wit of its commander could have recovered any of the souls aboard from that dire circumstance.

At the same time as they had received this news, they had learned that the Admiral hoped to reassemble the fleet at the Tortuga soundings, but Gabriel knew that his hull was in no condition to carry on with the expedition, and signaled back that they were making for the safety of port. Most of all, as the ship made its way under a crystalline blue sky and light, sweet breezes in the wake of the tempest, Gabriel was eager to relinquish his command and return to his duties belowdecks, should his arm heal sufficiently.

Looking about the harbor, he could see that most of the rest of the fleet had come to similar conclusions and were already jockeying for position near the great shipyards to patch their hurts and resupply the men and materiel that had been lost. He noted that the Admiral's flagship was not among those gathered, and hoped that the calamity that had overtaken the fleet had not claimed its leaders.

Past the thicket of improvised jury-masts on damaged ships, the town gleamed prettily in the sunlight, and he wondered idly whether he would have time to make his way to the cathedral to give his confession, or whether he would be kept fully engaged in the effort to make his ship seaworthy to stand for Pensacola as soon as possible. He fervently hoped that if this were to be the case, that the Admiralty would find someone else to carry the burden of her command.

The ship found its anchor, and Gabriel summoned Roger to join him as they clambered down into the launch and went ashore to report to the commander at *la Cabaña*. The task was awkward for him, with only one usable arm, and he could see that Roger was moving stiffly as well, the edge of a still-purpled bruise visible over his collar.

They made their way to the relative security of their seats in the middle of the launch, and the two junior seamen detailed for the task pulled at their oars, and Gabriel was able to lean close in to Roger's ear, asking, "What do you think of the flagship's absence from these waters?"

Roger looked around at the harbor, taking in the diminished and shattered fleet arrayed about it. "I think that General Gálvez and the Admiral remain eager to get to Pensacola, before any more British reinforcements could arrive. They are likely reconnoitering its situation, and gathering up stragglers from the fleet."

Gabriel nodded, chuckling, "Success is assured now, though, since Gálvez has again lost his fleet to the wind and sea. With the severity of this most recent loss, he must have felt that the omens were even more in his favor than ever before."

Roger shot Gabriel a startled look and said, "Surely you do not think that the General welcomed the storm?"

Gabriel raised his good hand in a friendly, dismissive gesture. "No, not that he wished the storm upon us, but that once it struck the fleet, he must have chosen to regard it as secure proof that our side was favored in the contest to come at Pensacola."

Roger nodded in agreement. "I can just see him doing exactly that. *Dios mío*, but that man does not see any event as anything but a blessing." He smiled back at Gabriel, adding, "It is good to see you recovering your natural optimism as well. Serving as captain of your ship seems to suit you well, *mí amigo*."

Gabriel rolled his shoulders, as though testing the freedom of the warm air away from the ship. He winced as the motion disturbed his arm, still bound to his side. He shook his head. "I lack any ambition for command, my friend. I like too much the freedom to make decisions without the constant worry that they may cost dozens of good men their lives, should I be wrong." He nodded his head toward the rising walls of the approaching fortress and said, "I hope to emerge from there as a free man."

Looking back to read Roger's face, he added quietly, "I know that not all share my lack of enthusiasm for command. Shall I put in a word on your behalf?"

Roger looked up sharply at Gabriel, thinking for a moment before he answered, "I do not think that it is likely to make any particular difference in the general view that I may not be fully trusted, owing to my birth on the shores of that nation with which we now contest this sea."

He shrugged and said, "Since you are immune to the desire to raise your own flag, however, I do not see where it could do either one of us any harm. As much as I embrace the duties that I have been asked to discharge, I will confess that my heart yearns for the opportunity to prove myself capable of more."

Gabriel nodded back and placed his hand on Roger's unhurt shoulder. "Consider it done, then. Perhaps, if our little ship can be made sound again, you shall yet command her as she sails for Pensacola."

Roger grinned and answered, "Only if I may have the best quartermaster in the fleet aboard to ensure that my men are victualed and supplied."

Gabriel rolled his eyes in answer, but was spared the need to come up with a witty rejoinder by the call from the sailor at the front of the boat, "Mind your balance, we're grounding now." The prow scraped onto the shore, and both of the junior seamen jumped over the sides to pull it fully onto the beach.

As the launch settled onto the sand, Gabriel and Roger stood and made their way forward to disembark. After they stepped onto the sand, the two men shared a long look of mutual admiration, and then Gabriel nodded quickly in approval of his friend's visage, before turning to make his way to the gate of the fortress.

As he passed a construction site where, Roger had mentioned on their first visit to the city, a new palace for the Captains-General was being built, a reeking woman approached him, singing out with a leer, "Just a handful of coins will buy you all the treasures I have to offer." He glanced at her luridly painted face and averted his eyes from the display she then made of some of those treasures.

He brushed past her, saying, "I already know where my city of gold may be found, *gracias*."

She shrieked after him, "You would not be so hasty to pass by heaven, had you seen enough of hell."

Gabriel turned back to the prostitute and said, "Indeed, I have seen enough of hell in my days to recognize when *el diablo* is sending some new temptation to lure me there. Repent, good woman, and reclaim your place in the sun."

The breeze shifted and carried the stench of her unwashed body to him, only slightly masked by the sickly, fruity sweetness of her cheap perfume. He recoiled visibly at the mingled odors, and she made a rude gesture at him before turning to find some more likely customer.

Gabriel shook his head sadly and continued through the great iron gates of the fortress, making his way through the courtyard. He nodded to each of the soldiers standing guard along the way to the great door, where a bored-looking guard sat just visible through a small viewport. As he approached, the guard stood up languidly, saying, "Who are you, and what is your business at this place?"

Gabriel introduced himself, as the guard looked him over closely, adding, "I am here to report the return of my ship, late of the invasion fleet, to the Havana harbor."

The guard raised an eyebrow at him, but nodded, replying, "They will surely wish to speak with you without delay." Gabriel could hear the bolt to the door being drawn, and it opened with the protesting squeal of hinges gone too long without grease.

He entered into the dimly lit and close air of the sally port, and the guard closed and bolted the door behind him. Motioning to a straight-backed chair beside the door, the guard said, "Sit here. I will send a boy to tell them you are arrived."

The guard opened the door that led into the fortress, summoned a messenger, spoke quietly into his ear, and sent him away, then sat in his own chair at the other side of the entrance, pointedly ignoring Gabriel. As Gabriel waited, he began to wonder whether his actions had been reported ahead and found lacking in some particular. He went over in his mind the decisions that he'd made in bringing his ship back, and thought about all of the alternatives that he'd passed over along the way.

Was there any point at which he could have saved more of his crew from injury and death? Were there doubts about the stowage of gear and supplies prior to the captain's demise? Did the commanders who sat safe in their homes in Havana believe that he should have rejoined the fleet, pushing his already exhausted crew to somehow make his ship ready?

After what seemed an eternity, the messenger returned and spoke to the guard, again too quietly for Gabriel to make out what was said. As the boy relayed his message, the guard looked up sharply at Gabriel and said, "You are to accompany the messenger to meet with the commanders and make your report."

He stood and bowed slightly to Gabriel, his eyes reflecting more regard than before. Gabriel stood and returned the bow, and followed the messenger, now feeling utterly mystified. As they walked down the long, arched corridors into the depths of the fortress, his mind was awhirl with worry and confusion.

Finally, the boy stopped at the entrance to a long room, comparatively dazzling in the light that streamed through windows all along its wall. A grave-looking man in uniform sat at his table, a plate of meat and bread sitting, ignored, at his elbow. The messenger boy called out, his voice high and clear, "Gabriel Llalandro Garcia y Cortez."

The officer waved the boy away and said wearily, "Come, *Señor* Garcia, and give me the report of your ship."

Gabriel had little direct experience of military courtesies, and was suddenly painfully aware that he appeared not in the uniform of an officer of His Catholic Majesty's Naval Services, but in the humble outfit of a working sailor. He did his best to approximate military bearing, though, as he approached the desk stiffly, and held himself at attention, staring at a fixed point above the officer's head as he recited, "Acting Captain Garcia of the troop transport *Numero Ocho*, at your command."

The officer looked up at Gabriel and nodded, replying, "Please, sit, and *por Dios*, relax." As Gabriel sat in the chair before his table that the officer gestured toward, he continued, "I presume that you have been pressed by events into a service that you could not anticipate?"

Gabriel nodded, still not quite able to release the tension that had built up between his shoulder blades. "Our captain and first mate were both taken in the storm, as my report will state. Both served with valor, and it is through their efforts that I had any ship at all to bring back to harbor."

Without betraying any emotion, the officer said, "I trust that your report will also summarize for the *Junta de Generales* the troops and supplies that you were able to preserve?"

Gabriel nodded again, replying, "Our losses were but moderate, though we have many injuries and the men are exhausted with the effort of keeping the ship swimming. She is leaking badly, and we have been obliged to keep men at the pumps even now—" The officer raised his hand to interrupt, a grim expression on his face.

His voice tired, he said, "I am not concerned at this time with the details of your command, Captain. Every ship that has returned from being mauled by this storm has a similar story to tell, and I am only charged with assembling a sense of how soon General Gálvez can gather the necessary forces to complete his project at Pensacola . . . while defending Mobile and New Orleans from the danger of the British retaking them, which he is constantly warning us about . . . but now I am discussing matters that do not concern you; my apologies."

The officer sighed. "We will, of course, make the docks and stores of the shipyard available to repair and reprovision your ship. You mentioned that you lost all of your superior officers to the storm; we can recruit replacements to serve under you, unless you have picked men among your own crew already?"

Gabriel shook his head slightly. "I am not certain that I am fit to serve even as a quartermaster, sir, in light of my injuries, much less as a captain. I should be glad for the opportunity to serve under any officers that you might see fit to supply my ship with, though there is a member of my crew whom I believe to be worthy of consideration."

The officer looked at Gabriel expectantly, an expression of mild surprise in his eyes, and Gabriel continued, "My ship's master is a man of uncommon ability, though he has been denied the opportunity to serve, owing to the accident of his birth. He is of British origins, though he has loyalty now only to King Carlos, and he would welcome the chance to demonstrate his fealty by service in command."

The officer gave him a look of skepticism and said, "It would go poorly for us all, should such a man be placed in a position of trust, only later to turn out not to have deserved that honor."

Gabriel nodded, turning the gesture into a sitting bow to the officer. "I would vouch for this man, and have trusted him with my very life. General Gálvez, too, was enough satisfied with his trustworthiness to have used him as a translator during his negotiations at Mobile."

The officer scowled and nodded to himself, muttering, "Gálvez knows little of the caution that we wish to see exercised, but he does seem to be a good judge of a man's character in most cases."

He shook his head and said, "Again, however, this is not a matter of concern to you." He chewed his lip for a moment. "As for yourself, I will recommend that we relieve you of your command until such time as you are again fit for duty. At that time, we will determine how best to make use of your services, should you wish to continue to serve."

His eyes narrowed and he looked at Gabriel shrewdly. "What is your background, *Señor* Garcia? How do you come to be in the service of the King?"

"Until last year, I was no more than a quartermaster in a merchant ship working the Mississippi River. I volunteered to assist the Governor's defense of New Orleans, and since then, it has been my honor to serve King Carlos and General Gálvez."

The officer nodded, something like approval creeping into his expression. "So, you know both the waters and the people of the Mississippi and New Orleans?"

Puzzled, Gabriel nodded slowly in reply, adding, "I have some particular friends and men whom I esteem greatly among those people, yes. But in what way could that apply to my service to the General or the King?"

The officer raised a hand in placation, saying, "Perhaps not in any way, but it is good to know of as much as we can of your capacities as we ponder your further duties. Please, tell me what you know of the river trade?"

Gabriel summarized, "In the greatest part, I have spent my working years in that trade below the decks of one small river cargo ship or another. I have traveled as far up the river as the trading post at Saint Louis, but the last time I was there would have been even before the American colonies rebelled against the British Crown."

Nodding with enthusiasm, the officer said, "You have likely not yet heard of the recent action there, but this past spring, the British attempted to take that town, coming down the river from the north with a band of howling savages. Our men beat them back, but it cost us dear."

He put his chin in his hand and said, almost more to himself than to Gabriel, "You would not have known Governor Leyba, as he was only appointed a couple of years ago." Gabriel shook his head to agree that he had no knowledge of the name, and the officer continued, "His loss was a sad one, as he showed great energy and creativity in his defense of that town."

Laying his hands back down on the desk and sitting up straight, he said, "In any event, the town remains in our hands, but you have no experience of it anyway, so it matters not. Have you traveled the Gulf coast much prior to your service to General Gálvez?"

Gabriel shrugged. "Trade with the British in East-Florida was never much, but I have been as far west as *el Orcoquisac*, before it was abandoned, but that was only because their regular supply ship was sent—"

Again, the officer raised his hand to stop Gabriel, shaking his head. "You know the Mississippi River, and New Orleans best, then?"

Gabriel nodded. "I have spent more time in New Orleans than in most places, *es verdad*."

The officer, lost in thought now, nodded in reply and stood up, prompting Gabriel to stand as well. "Very well. When you have completed your report, you may send it by messenger. Have you lodgings arranged in the city yet?"

"I do not, as I did not dare to assume that I would know what I might be called upon to do upon my report to you."

"A prudent decision, but as your command is relieved, you should remove your effects from the ship; it is the common practice of the service, as you may appreciate." Taking note, as if for the first time, of Gabriel's close-slung arm, the officer said, apparently with real interest, "What is the nature of your injury, and with whom have you consulted for its treatment?"

Gabriel shrugged as well as he could and answered, "It is an unreduced fracture of the bones of my lower arm, and my ship's doctor declared it beyond his skills, other than to offer me a bitter draught for it that he said would aid the bones. If you might recommend a man who is reluctant with the saw, but otherwise skilled, I would be most grateful."

The officer made an expression of thoughtful frustration, saying, "Alas, most men one encounters in the services are all too happy to have your arm or leg off, and none too skilled at making them straight and well. You might ask around at the yards, though, as they have their share of fractures and injuries, and doubtless know who can be trusted."

Bowing slightly to Gabriel, the officer said, "I wish you joy in your safe return to the land, and pray for your speedy recovery."

Gabriel returned the bow, and walked crisply out of the room, finding the boy still waiting for him at the entrance. Without a word, the messenger led him back to the guard at the entrance, who looked up tiredly from the piece of wood he was carving.

"He took longer with you than he does with most," the guard commented, as he set down his handiwork and moved to the door. "You must have had an interesting time of it."

Whether the man spoke of Gabriel's audience with the officer, or his travels since the storm was unclear, but in either case, Gabriel didn't think that it was his place to speak to this man, so he only nodded and smiled in affirmation. The guard shrugged and worked the bolt in the gate, and pushed it open, standing aside to let Gabriel exit.

After he passed through the portal, Gabriel turned and asked, "Can you recommend clean, inexpensive lodgings? I am to stay ashore until I am required, but I know nothing of this town."

The guard's forehead wrinkled in thought as Gabriel imagined him weighing the referral payments on offer from the various different boarding-houses. He finally said, "If you were to inquire for *el Cabalo Real* once you get to the cathedral district, someone can probably send you in the right direction."

Gabriel nodded in gratitude and made his way back to the launch, noting with a frown that the woman who had accosted him was busily haggling with another potential customer as he passed. At the shore, when he saw Roger's familiar form reclined across the benches of the launch, his hat pulled over his eyes to provide some shade for his nap, Gabriel could not help but grin.

"*Hola, mí capitán,*" he called out to his friend, startling the sleeping man, who attempted to jump to his feet, knocking his hat over the side and into the sand just above the waves lapping at the shore.

With a sour glance over the gunwale at the hat, Roger called back, "I am no man's captain, unless you bring me unexpected news from *la Cabaña.*"

Smiling and handing the sand-encrusted hat up to his friend, Gabriel said, "Not certain news, no, but I am relieved of my command due to my injury, and I have asked that they consider you as a fit replacement."

Roger bowed in gratitude, as he brushed sand from the hat and placed it back onto his head. "I am grateful for your kindness, *mí capitán,*" he said, placing particular stress on the first word. "What orders have you received at this time?"

"I am to shift my effects to shore and await further assignments while this heals," Gabriel said, frowning and tossing his chin in the direction of his bound-up arm.

"Well, then, I can be of service to you at least this one more time," Roger replied, offering his hand to his friend to board the launch. "I should think it prudent to join you ashore, until they have made up their minds whether I am the man they want to command even a half-sunken, waddling troop transport."

Chapter 22

The sea air, fresh off the open Gulf, was a nice change from the fetid quarters Gabriel had found in Havana. He shifted on his feet, wincing slightly as the motion jostled his arm.

The dock men had been able to recommend a surgeon, a man well-versed in the most modern techniques and theories, to look at the fracture. Gabriel still felt a wave of faintness and nausea at the memory of the unique quality of pain that the grey-bearded, grim little man had inflicted upon him.

Where the bones had begun to knit together, but out of all alignment with one another, the physician had gritted his brown-stained teeth together with effort, and had applied sufficient force to un-knit, and then realign them. Gabriel had never quite passed out throughout the procedure, but he had shouted himself hoarse, and his memory of the afternoon was, mercifully, already faded and dim.

Despite the agony of the treatment, though, Gabriel was grateful for the fact that he still had his hand, and could even begin to start moving it, which had been impossible before the fracture had been properly treated. Soon, he hoped, he'd be able to remove it from the sling, and perhaps, one day, to use it again.

In the meantime, he was on watch duty on a small cutter making its way swiftly toward the garrison at New Orleans, keeping an eye on the horizon for the telltale white flash of sails. There had been nothing but the occasional billowing thunderclouds in the distance in the days since Cuba sank below the horizon, the swift little craft's wake forming a straight, white furrow in the waters behind them.

Gabriel found himself hoping on more than one occasion that they might set a course that took them within view of the shore, and further from the storms, trivial though they might turn out to be. By any reckoning, he thought that he had had enough of rough weather to last all of his life.

Today, though, the horizon was clear and sharp in all quarters, marred by neither sail nor storm, nor any hint of land. They sailed close to the sweet, unfailing wind, which pushed them almost directly toward New Orleans, as if God Himself wanted them to arrive quickly, both to speed the delivery of the messages Gabriel carried, and to return Gabriel to the village where Carlotta awaited him.

Gabriel patted the sealed packet he had been instructed to deliver into the hand of the garrison commander at New Orleans, as his final duty to the King. His orders from *la Cabaña* had released him from further service, owing to his extreme sacrifices and serious injuries. He could not help but wonder if he had been judged wanting in courage for his decision to bring the troop carrier back to Havana, but the return of the flagship itself, along with the remnants of the rest of the fleet, gave him some comfort on that question.

While the fleet underwent repairs and the men of the invasion force recovered themselves from their ordeal at sea, word spread through the town of the failed British attempt at re-taking

Mobile through an overland attack from Pensacola. Bold though the stroke had been, the resolve of the Spanish defenders had sent them back without their commander, and it was a constant topic of discussion what the British might do next.

Some forces had been dispatched from Havana to reinforce Mobile, and Gabriel's old command, the patched-up *Ocho*, had been among those ordered to transport troops.

His last conversation with Roger before his departure had been bittersweet, as that worthy man's service did not seem to have been well-rewarded, either; he was ordered to remain as ship's master, under a captain whose ship had sunk at its moorings after he got it into the harbor.

Roger had taken a long pull at a half-empty bottle, saying, "I tell you, *mí amigo*, I am to remain a ship's master until the end of my days, as there is no nation on the seas that will now trust me with command of one of its ships."

Gabriel could smell the rum on his disappointed friend's breath, but kept his counsel on that point, instead answering, "I am grieved to hear of this, Roger, but let me assure you that your friendship, and your service under my limited command, are not so lightly valued."

Roger grimaced. "It is but frustrating to feel truly a part of no nation afloat, under threat of a noose from my birth country, and always under a cloud of suspicion, no matter how lightly phrased, from the country I now serve." He'd shaken his head, dispelling his sour mood as well as he was able. "I hear, though, that you are to return to your Carlotta, about whom I have heard so much."

Gabriel shrugged. "If she has waited for me these months away—indeed, it has been nearly a year since I left." Shrugging again, he added, "We were not pledged to one another when I left, and she was still fresh in grief for the loss of her father and her first husband. Much can change in a woman's heart under such circumstances."

"Have faith, my old friend," Roger said, offering the bottle to Gabriel's expected half-smile and upraised hand of grateful refusal. "Ah, I know you won't take any of the rum, but you should take my words anyway. Carlotta—and her father—saved you, and you have saved them. That will not be lightly forgotten, and your reward awaits." Roger upended the bottle then, finishing it, and stood with remarkable steadiness. "I must report to my ship, as we sail with the tide. God's love go with you, *mi amigo.*"

Gabriel stood and embraced his friend. "And with you."

Reflecting on the conversation with Roger, Gabriel found himself looking eagerly for the first hint of the shore where Carlotta was. He knew that it would be another day at least before they raised land, but he willed the horizon to yield its first hint of home as soon as possible.

He frowned at the thought, feeling the shift in his feelings as a visceral thing. Had he ever truly had a place he considered home before? He had served on ships for so long that he scarcely remembered what it was to have a home on land. To be sure, he'd nearly always been within sight of land—perhaps that was the source of his disquiet now?—but since his boyhood, there had not been a single spot on Earth that called to him when he was away from it.

And yet, he felt suddenly certain that regardless of Carlotta's feelings for him upon his return, he would be well-satisfied to settle down among the villagers and make his life there. He knew that he could never return to the world of cordage and stowage, barrels and crates, even if his arm returned to its former strength.

Of course, he knew well that life ashore was no less demanding, though in different ways. There would be difficulties in any path that he took, and that thought cheered him, as he knew that whatever challenges might appear, he could overcome them.

Looking out beyond the prow of the cutter, the quality of the light was such that the demarcation between sky and sea was indistinct, and the sails pushed them toward a horizon that was without limit. He nodded to himself, satisfied. Tomorrow would bring landfall, and soon after, resolution to the questions of his heart.

Chapter 23

A letter from far-off Pensacola was a rare thing, and Gabriel sat in a bit of shade re-reading and pondering its content once again. Though the news of Spanish victory over the British had reached his ears some months past, it was of particular interest to read a familiar voice recount the events that had led up to it.

Roger's handwriting was nearly as exuberant as his words, as he related the outright heroism that General Gálvez had shown in the attack on the British colonial capitol. The fleet had sailed without complication from Havana, arriving to find another challenging passage into an unfriendly bay.

Though Roger did not come right out and call the Admiral shy of the danger, he did write that he thought that the naval officer and the General had nearly come to blows over the tactics they would follow to make their approach. Ultimately, Gálvez had personally taken station on the quarterdeck of his ship to guide it through the channel, heedless of the danger of British musketry and cannon fire, even as it struck at the rigging. Afterward, there was even a rumor that one of the naval commanders had challenged him to a duel.

Reinforced by troops sent from Mobile and New Orleans, Gálvez had again benefitted from intelligence provided by a deserter from the British lines, and learned where the powder magazine within the fort lay. A fortuitous shot right through the door of the magazine triggered a catastrophic explosion—Roger wrote that he still did not have the hearing back in his right ear—and the British were forced to surrender the next day.

Roger wrote that while he was not at liberty to say very much specifically, he expected to be dispatched with Gálvez' fleet to Jamaica next, to continue the Spanish project of taking as much of King George's American holdings as possible under the flag of their sovereign.

Once again, Gabriel laughed aloud at the final line of Roger's letter—"You will be gratified to know that you may address return correspondence to me via the *Junta de Generales* in Havana, as Captain Rogers of the *Ocho*." The word "Captain" was emphatically underlined and written twice as large as any other on the page, and Gabriel could feel in his heart the joy those few letters on the page contained.

Carlotta called out to him, and Gabriel turned toward her, and laughed aloud as his son took a tottering step, spanning the gap between Carlotta's knee and his outstretched arms in a single, wobbling stride, a joyful grin illuminating his face. He scooped the boy up in his arms, crying, "Ah, my little Salvador, I knew you could do it!"

Looking up from the giggling baby to his wife's serene smile, Gabriel returned her smile and closed his eyes, facing into the sunshine and smelling the warm breeze coming in from the ocean. He had found his answers, and needed nothing more.

Also in Audiobook

Many readers love the experience of turning the pages in a paper book such as the one you hold in your hands. Others enjoy hearing a skilled narrator tell them a story, bringing the words on the page to life.

Brief Candle Press has arranged to have *The Wind* produced as a high-quality audiobook, and you can listen to a sample and learn where to purchase it in that form by scanning the QR code below with your phone, tablet, or other device, or going to the Web address shown.

Happy listening!

bit.ly/TheWindAudio

Historical Notes

S ometimes, one comes across actual historical events that are so remarkable and compelling that it seems unbelievable that they haven't already been the topic of dozens of novels and movies.

The scenes I depict in *The Wind* contain just such a sequence of events: three campaigns, three storms, three victories.

Of course, they took place at the periphery of the American Revolution, in a part of the overall war that featured primarily European powers fighting for their own interests on our shores. However, the strategic impact of Gálvez' sweep through the British holdings on the Gulf Coast was significant to the overall success of our Revolution.

Had he failed to close down English access to the Mississippi, it may well have been possible for the British to have introduced reinforcements overland from the West, squeezing Patriot forces when they needed maneuvering room in their running battles up through the South, on their way to victory at Yorktown.

Too, Gálvez likely kept the British Navy occupied preparing for the possibility of further expeditions out from Florida—both of the colonies of West and East Florida were ceded to Spain following the British defeat at Pensacola—which hindered their ability to keep the French away from American waters, which was also key to the victory at Yorktown.

While Gálvez has long languished in popular histories of the American Revolution, he is memorialized in the name of one major American city—Galveston, Texas—and he was recently accorded the honor of being among the very few individuals to have honorary citizenship in the United States of America conferred upon him. Finally, his portrait has finally been hung at the U.S. Capitol, 231 years after the Congress passed a resolution ordering that it be "placed in the room in which Congress meets," and the Galveston chapter of the Sons of the American Revolution is working on having a statue placed in that city to commemorate its namesake.

In our traditional focus on the Boston–New-York–Philadelphia nexus of the American Revolution, we lose sight of some of the most remarkable heroes of that struggle, and I am glad to be able to contribute in some small way to rectifying that oversight.

Three cheers for Bernardo de Gálvez y Madrid!

Acknowledgements

Some years ago, soon after the publication of *The Prize*, I was chatting with John Heppner, one of my father's friends. He asked whether I planned to write about Florida. I had to stop for a moment—was Florida even a British colony? I had to confess that I was entirely ignorant of Florida's role in the American Revolution . . . which, of course, meant that it was a rich opportunity to find some untold stories of that time to share with my readers. This novel is the outcome of that conversation, and I acknowledge with gratitude the debt that I owe to John for planting the seed.

I also want to thank the many researchers who kept the remarkable story Bernardo de Gálvez alive through the years, with particular attention to Thomas Fleming for his thorough and highly approachable article in *American Heritage Magazine*, which gave me many of the hints I needed to flesh out the history behind this story. I am honored, too, to be a fellow contributor with him to the Journal of the American Revolution, which may be found at allthingsliberty.com.

I'd also like to acknowledge the contributions of my editor, Ingrid Bevz of Green Ink Proofreading, whose many helpful suggestions and corrections improved this novel greatly. Errors, of course, remain my own.

Thank You

I deeply appreciate you spending the past couple of hundred pages with the characters and events of a world long past, yet hopefully relevant today.

If you enjoyed this book, I'd also be grateful for a kind review on your favorite bookseller's Web site or social media outlet. Word of mouth is the best way to make me successful, so that I can bring you even more high-quality stories of bygone times.

I'd love to hear directly from you, too—feel free to reach out to me via my Facebook page, Twitter feed or Web site, and let me know what you liked, and what you would like me to work on more.

Again, thank you for reading, for telling your friends about this book, for giving it as a gift or dropping off a copy in your favorite classroom or library. With your support and encouragement, we'll find even more times and places to explore together.

larsdhhedbor.com
Facebook: LarsDHHedbor
@LarsDHHedbor on Twitter

Enjoy a preview of the next book in the
Tales From a Revolution series:

The Darkness

George rubbed his hands together, in an effort to warm them in the morning chill. The past season of snow and ice seemed to be grudgingly releasing its hold on the island, and he'd heard his parents comment on multiple occasions during the dark months that it had been the hardest winter they could remember. He was waiting by the shoreline for Lemuel, who was to bring him to town for the day, with a list of items his mother desired him to purchase for the coming season.

The sun had risen now, with the promise of warmth later in the day, but a dense line of trees stood along the ridge above the beach where his brother was to meet him, and in their shadow, it was still cold enough that he could see his breath.

He could hear a rooster crowing from somewhere behind him, announcing that daybreak had come to his part of the island, and in the distance, he could hear a hound of some sort howling mournfully. It was probably Lemuel's dog, bereft at being left behind while its master went off on some errand without him.

Just then, the prow of Lemuel's boat swung into view around the entrance to the cove, and George called out to him.

"Hullo, Lemuel!"

"Good morning to you, George!" Lemuel's voice carried cheerfully across the cold water. As he drew closer, he said, "You have Mother's list?"

"Yes, naturally, and the money that Father provided to pay for what she requires."

Lemuel strained at the oars for a few more strokes, and as the boat scraped onto the shore, he said, panting, "Then I pray that we will be able to secure the items we need. Come, jump aboard."

George stepped onto the boat with one foot, and pushed it off with the other before scrambling into his seat beside Lemuel, as the boat drifted silently into the cove. Both took a moment to adjust the oars so that they were placed for two oarsmen instead of one, and at a nod from Lemuel, they began pulling in unison.

Their labor precluded much conversation, until they emerged from the lee of the island, and the prevailing breeze could reach them. The sight of the sail rising under Lemuel's experienced hands, and then filling with wind to hurry them on their way made George's heart glad, and Lemuel's quiet assurance as he adjusted the sail and set the tiller into the water that sluiced by the side of the boat filled him with admiration. He wondered whether he might ever gain the ability to conduct himself on the water with such skill.

Lemuel did not ask for his help, and George did not offer it—it was a simple craft, designed to be sailed by one person, and George knew from experience that extra hands would only confuse the process of managing the sail and tiller.

This left George free to ponder the shoreline as they approached, marred as it was by the unwelcome intrusion of the fortifications that the British had thrown up upon seizing this area the prior year.

It had mushroomed, seemingly overnight, from a set of rude trenches and earthworks, to fully-realized fort, with low-slung timber walls punctuated with high blockhouses at each corner. The whole affair crouched, sullen and ominous over the town as a silent threat, and the British flag on its staff served as a daily rebuke to all those who wished that the King would tend to his own affairs, and leave this small settlement in peace.

Lemuel steered the boat around the peninsula on which the fort stood, and as they passed into the shadow of the structure, the chill of the morning reasserted itself. They emerged back into the sun as they sailed past the narrow neck of land that connected it to the mainland, which was interrupted with additional walls and defenses. Lemuel furled the sail as they approached the land, calling out to George, "Get ready on the oars, now."

George centered himself between them, and as Lemuel managed the tiller, he began pulling at the oars to keep their momentum toward shore going.

His brother picked the spot on the shore where he wanted to land the boat, and said, "Just a bit more, George . . . good, you can stop rowing now."

The gravel of the beach grated underneath the boat, and George laid the oars back along the sides of the boat and stood, stepping over the side of the prow to drag it further ashore. Lemuel joined him, and the two brothers pulled the small craft well out of reach of the waves.

"Tide's going out soon, and we'll be back before it comes up this far again," Lemuel said, and George nodded in reply. "Shall we go to the mercantile together, and then attend to the rest of our errands individually?"

"That suits my purposes," George answered, and they set off.

The village was relatively quiet, but a few townspeople were in evidence, going about their daily affairs with friendly smiles and familiar nods to the two young men.

They reached the mercantile, and they each in turn presented their shopping lists to Mr. Jones, who had bought out the prior owner of the shop with the arrival of the British. Mr. Rutherford, who had sold it, was said to have joined up with the rebels at Machias, further up the coast, where the Americans had a stronghold.

Jones didn't go for all that political intrigue, and was well satisfied to do business with all comers, British and Americans alike. Some of the rebel sympathizers in town avoided his store, but like most people, George and Lemuel gritted their teeth and bought what they needed from him.

George's pile of goods was quite a bit heftier than Lemuel's, when they were finished, but he gathered it all into a sack and said, "Mr. Jones, I trust that we may leave these with you for safekeeping, until we have finished with my other business in town, and we are ready to return home?"

"Of course," said the merchant, a knowing smile on his face. "Can't leave goods unattended these days, what with all the lawlessness and disruption lately in these parts."

Lemuel smiled in reply, perhaps a bit cooler than Jones, and said, "Indeed, with our visitors about, any peculiar thing could happen to unguarded valuables."

The other man's smile stiffened a touch, and he nodded politely. "I'll keep them under my personal observation until you are ready to collect them."

George nodded to him, and as the brothers left the mercantile, he hissed at Lemuel, "Why did you prod him so?"

Lemuel gave George a grim look and said, "I'll not make the British occupation of this district any more easy than it absolutely must be. They are interlopers in this colony, and those who sympathize with them, too. I mean to make him uncomfortable."

"You'll be reported as a rebel supporter."

"Nay, I am most careful to not give them cause to act." He shrugged. "And if he reports me, let him. They'll find nothing in examining me."

"Or Beatrice?"

Lemuel's face grew stormy. "They'll leave my wife out of it entirely, if they have any care for their skins."

"'Tis your skin at risk, more than theirs." George motioned up the hill at the fort. "One man can hardly argue with that."

Lemuel gave George a stubborn grimace, but he did not answer, instead pausing for a moment before saying, "I'll meet you back here at around noontime."

George nodded and said, "I'll keep an eye on the sun." Without another word, the brothers parted, Lemuel to attend to some business he'd not chosen to elaborate upon, and George to see about making arrangements to trade with a local trapper.

He entered a narrow alley between two houses, a shortcut he preferred over walking the long way around the long line of houses and businesses. As he entered the shadowed space where the eaves from the two buildings nearly met, he heard a girlish shriek, followed by what sounded like a hand striking bare flesh, and a grunt of surprise.

Cautiously, George proceeded toward the source of the noise, feeling his heartbeat pound in his ears. Coming around the corner in a crouch, he saw a young woman standing over the writhing form in the uniform of a British soldier.

She was facing away from George, and had not heard his approach, and he was surprised to see her draw her foot back and kick the soldier on the chin, saying in a low, angry voice, "That'll serve you for thinking that you can just take of any Colonial girl whom you fancy." George wasn't sure, but he thought he heard the crack of bone breaking when her boot struck the man's face.

He had no time to wonder, though, as the girl turned to leave and caught sight of him. She gave out another small shriek, and covered her mouth in surprise, her eyes narrowing in anger.

"Are you in league with this devil, then?" she asked, advancing on George with a menacing manner.

Despite himself, he found that he was frightened for his safety—this was obviously someone to reckon with. "Nay, I just heard your exclamation a moment ago, and came to see whether you needed any assistance." He gestured at the now-still figure on the ground behind her and added, "I can see now that you do not."

Her posture softened, and shoulders sagged as she said, "Thank God. I did not relish fighting off another." She approached, looking smaller and more vulnerable than she had a moment before, and George could see that she was shaking visibly.

He felt the urge to take her into a comforting embrace, but stifled that impulse, saying, "We had best be elsewhere when he awakes. I think you broke his jaw, and the garrison here will not look kindly on one of their own being so injured in town, no matter the circumstances."

She gasped slightly and took his elbow in her hand, guiding

him around the far corner of the building he'd just passed by. "Come quickly, then, and let us tell my mother what has happened. She will know what to do."

Though he had no part in her predicament, George felt moved to help her if he could, and followed at a jog behind her as she pointed the way through the maze of houses in the village center. They emerged back onto the main road, and she released his elbow, slowing to a more normal pace, as there were more people were moving about than had been earlier in the day.

A patrol of four British soldiers was among those on the street, and for an instance, George felt as though his heart had stopped in his chest. The girl spotted them, too, and turned as casually as she could to George, leaned in toward him, and said in an urgent whisper, "Kiss my cheek."

George tried to hide his startled expression, as he realized what she was trying to do, and mustered the courage to give her a quick, chaste buss. Though the kiss might have been faked, the blush that spread over his face afterward was completely authentic.

The brief contact between his lips and the petal-soft skin of her face lasted for only the briefest of instants, and yet it seemed as though the entire morning ran its course before the connection between them ended.

Acting her role a bit too convincingly, the girl gave him a coquettish little smile and turned away, her skirts swirling about her feet as she strode away. He hazarded a glance up and down the street, and was somehow shocked to find that nobody else present—including the bored soldiers—seemed to have noticed the moment at all.

Shaking his head to clear his thoughts, George willed his

breathing to slow, even as he could feel his cheeks still burning, and turned away from the patrol to find a more roundabout path to his meeting with the trapper.

As he walked down the road with his ears abuzz, he shook his head at the knowledge that he didn't know where the girl had gone to seek refuge with her mother. Indeed, although the warmth of her cheek was etched into his memory, he realized that he hadn't even learned her name.

Look for The Darkness: Tales From a Revolution - Maine at your favorite booksellers.